Souls in the Twilight

Souls in the Twilight

STORIES OF LOSS

ROGER SCRUTON

BEAUFORT
BOOKS

SOULS IN THE TWILIGHT

Library of Congress Cataloging-in-Publication Data on File

Paperback: 9780825308840
Ebook: 9780825307720

For inquiries about volume orders, please contact:
Beaufort Books
27 West 20th Street, Suite 1102
New York, NY 10011
sales@beaufortbooks.com

Published in the United States by Beaufort Books
www.beaufortbooks.com

Distributed by Midpoint Trade Books
www.midpointtrade.com

Book designed by Mark Karis

Printed in the United States of America

CONTENTS

PREFACE

These stories, written over a decade, describe a world that the Internet has yet to tear apart, and characters whose search for meaning sends no ripples into cyberspace. The narratives start, and end, in England. But the significant times and places, whether real or imaginary, are always elsewhere.

MALMESBURY, DECEMBER 2017

WE TAKE THE TRAIN FROM LIVERPOOL STREET. It's my favourite station: all light and space, and now with the shops and cafés, and the people in their city clothes. The girls so smart and clean, like they've just stepped out of adverts. Great! I borrow some cash from Fareed and buy an Oasis T-shirt, the one with the limousine in the swimming pool. It's for the journey home. The girl smiles at me as she wraps it up, and when I ask, she gives me her phone number. Cool! Fareed buys a tie and a posh jacket in blue cotton, but she doesn't smile at him. She's called Jenny, short for Jennifer maybe.

It's the middle of the morning and the train is empty. I like trains: I like the people-smell, the soft seats, the big windows, and the other lives carried next to yours, only not quite touching. And just sitting there, with nothing to do and no one to trouble you! Great! Back home, Abba says, the trains are pulled by steam engines, smoke and smut in your eyes and nowhere to sit, wooden seats smothered by the *bibis* wrapped in black, people shouting and quarrelling, and long stops between stations where no one can get off and the sun roars down like a flame-thrower. He used to go every week to Algiers on the big train—the *qitar kabir*—and the way he says the words makes me think of a huge guitar, strumming quietly, and the long train snaking through the desert.

Blue sky, spring sunshine, a clear light on the chimney stacks as we speed through Finsbury Park. Each tile on the roofs, each little panel of brickwork, picked out by sun and shadow. I love those queer houses—Edwardian, according to Abba—sash windows, terra-cotta doorways, sturdy chimneys like bread-ovens. Abba likes them too, and when he gets an extension-job for an Edwardian house, he goes down to the reclamation centre at the Elephant, searching for glazed bricks and stained-glass panels, so that everything will look like it's always been there. He's like that, Abba: *wafi*, the servant of Allah and his work.

We pass a big house with parkland and a lake: beautiful, like a dream. And then more suburbs, some factories, marshy wasteland full of rusting cars and rubbish, and then a mosque—just look at it, four great minarets suddenly pricking the sky above a row of tired old houses and grubby washing-lines! I feel a stab of joy and I can't stop myself from laughing aloud. Fareed frowns at me.

"Yusuf! Be discreet!" he says, in a whisper.

"But there's no one else on the train!"

"All the same..."

He looks at me as he did six months ago, when he gave that lecture on Ami's people and what they lost, and how I had promised Ami revenge when she was dying. As though I need reminding. I mean it's only common sense. I begin to recite the Surah of the Sun, whose light pours over those minarets and washes them so clean and white in the morning sky.

wa ash-shams wa duhaaha,

wa al-qamar idha talaaha...

But I forget the rest and feel annoyed with myself. Fareed goes on giving me his solemn frown. You can't deny that Fareed is good-looking in his Egyptian way, with those almond eyes and chiselled nostrils, and the soft brown hair always blowing this way and that across his forehead. He reminds me of Omar Sharif in *Lawrence of Arabia*. And when he frowns his whole face seems to pucker, as though someone were gripping it from behind at a point in the centre of the neck. It's a really dignified frown, a super-frown, the frown of an angel suddenly looking down at you out of the clouds. So I feel annoyed with myself and turn again to the window. There are churches now, with their spires of chiselled stone, and here and there a block of flats rising above the tiled roof-tops. They remind me of those seaside postcards that make Abba laugh, I don't know why, with hideous fat-thighed women paddling in shallow water. How strange the world is, and how full of signs!

Then, all of a sudden, we're there: a little station with two narrow platforms and an old booking office in brick, boarded up now, and covered over with posters. A couple of blacks are standing on the platform and glare at us. There's a girl too, beautiful, with blond hair and tight trousers, who is sitting on a bench reading a book. She doesn't look up, and I can tell from her eyelashes that not looking up is a policy. Sometimes you want to touch people, to make them know you are on their side. That's how it is with me! But of course I just walk on as though I hadn't noticed her.

The sun is warm on my face. I am really looking forward to changing into the T-shirt with the drowned limousine. Fareed strides on, very serious, very determined, while I want to linger here and there, to look into the strange gardens, many of them already with flowers. The houses are such a muddle!—some with pebble-dash veneer and metal-frame windows, some with stone porches and stained-glass fanlights, some tall and swanky with high windows and witch-cap towers. And all glowing in this fantastic sunlight, like a vision. Amazing! Up high there's a plane; it catches the sunlight and shines like fire. I stand to watch it, shielding my eyes: a flaming sword in the sky. The sky opens to let it pass and then closes behind it, so neat and seamless and pure. Days like this you feel able to fly, up among the angels and looking down on the world. This is the bright forenoon in the surah of the forenoon, the dawn in the surah of the dawn! There was this fantastic poem we learned at school: "he who kisses the joy as it flies / Lives in eternity's sunrise." That's how to live!

"Hurry, they're waiting!"

Fareed's voice calling me to order: nothing new in that. You have to admire Fareed. He studies the world, finds his place in it, is always exactly where he should be at the time required. Compared with him I'm a bum and a layabout. Except for helping Abba, I've never had a job; never turn up for Friday prayers except in Ramadan; never start the day with a clear agenda—except for this day, the great day, the day when it's all going to happen and Ami will at last forgive me. I could dawdle in these streets all morning: Fareed makes sure I am going somewhere, moving on, making waves. Thanks, Fareed: my hero!

There's this fantastic cat just sitting on top of a gate-post, a kind of greenish-gold colour with burning orange eyes like traffic lights. It watches me as I pass and when I put out a hand to stroke it, the cat starts up and boxes me off with its paw. We spar like old partners, like we've known each other for years. One of those electric milk-floats has stopped at the house next door, and there's the milkman in a black-and-white striped apron, manhandling bottles down the drive. I want to call out to him, to remind him—I mean to let him know that he isn't alone. It all seems so new, so fresh, so joyous. And then Fareed, turning round again and again, gesticulating impatiently, not wanting to shout my name.

We're there. What a disappointment! No garden, just a concrete yard with an old stone bowl that looks like a disused fountain. The rendering on the facade has been picked out in white paint, the window frames are turquoise: and this on a three-storey terrace house. I could just imagine what Abba would say: *souqi*, cheap and nasty! But then second thoughts: charitable thoughts. It's all so innocent, so neat and proud and tidy. Really it's like it should be, all simplicity and goodness. How brilliant of Fareed to discover these people!

An old grandfather opens the door. He has a thin white beard like a goat, and his watery eyes are grey and slightly unfocused. His hands on Fareed's shoulders are like polished bones and he seems to peer into the sky as he reaches up for Fareed to kiss him. His name is Anwar; he's from Baghdad and speaks with an accent. We're shown into the front room, crowded with furniture: low tables with mock lapis-lazuli tops and plastic legs in the shape of elephant trunks; mirrors framed by arabesques of gold plaster; divans covered in mock-silk and spread with bright red and gold carpets. On the walls framed verses from the Holy Koran in kufic script, and in one corner an enormous television raised on a gilded trestle and draped with a cloth of orange silk.

Now we're drinking mint tea and conversing with Anwar, his son Fadil, and Fadil's wife Zeynab, a fat lady in cheap English clothes, with a long dress of printed yellow flowers. How pretty the flowers are in the light from the window, and how I enjoy looking at Zeynab's face, with its dimpled cheeks shaped by laughter, and each black eye set like a jewel in its frame of black wrinkles. She's from Hama in Syria, and her brother died there, she tells us, when Hafiz el-Assad massacred the Muslim Brotherhood. "*Jabaan al-asad,*" she says, cowardly lion. They all like to play on Assad's name, as Abba does. How the conversation has come round to such a topic I don't know. But Zeynab tells the story cheerfully, as though granted her revenge, and Fareed is soon asking her about some cloth she wanted. One thing I really admire about Fareed is how practical he is; he will never miss a business opportunity, and knows how to turn friendship to profit and—what is even better—profit to friendship. His eyes light up as he bargains, and his questions begin to explore the feelings of the other party, pinning back layer after layer like a surgeon until the heart lies exposed. Zeynab is clearly loving it, and I am loving it too.

Fadil, however, is silent. He is a small, hunched man, with liquid eyes like his father and a greying moustache. Perhaps he is not in the best of health, because every now and then he shifts uncomfortably on his leather cushion and utters a small troubled sigh. Once, when Fareed nods in his direction, he nods back, as though confirming some secret deal between them. And often he turns in my direction, not to talk, but to survey me with a kind of quiet astonishment, as though not quite sure that I am here. I smile at him, and he smiles back. But that's all.

And then it happens. Without warning the door opens and the most beautiful girl in the world glides through it, like a spirit wafted on the air. She is smiling at me, from soft sand-coloured lips in a perfect oval face, and her dark eyes glow with interest. Fareed looks away. Maybe he doesn't want to see the spark that passes between us. Zeynab leans back happily and says

"Halima, come and meet Yusuf."

I jump to my feet as she approaches. The blood has drained from my face and my lips tremble. I search for words. And still she smiles, keeping her distance as she must, bowing slightly and crossing her hands on her breast. How not to look at her is all my effort: how not to defile her with my eyes or my words or my thoughts. Eventually I am able to call down Allah's blessing on her and hers. She bows again and looks up at me through her eyelashes. Then she lowers her arms, shows firm pointed breasts before turning quickly away and retreating to the door. She beckons to her mother to follow her, and in a moment the men are alone.

I stand trembling, like one who has received a vision. Everything that has been planned for this day ends in her. It is for Halima's sake that I will do it: she's the cause, the goal, the prize. I turn to her father who is again surveying me from astonished eyes.

"A lovely girl," I stutter. "You must have hopes for her."

He makes a serious face.

"Well, you know how it is. We shan't be throwing our treasure away."

I try to find words for her: *bint al-Hilaal* sounds cheap—it's the language of a marriage broker. She's not even a girl for me, but something holy, untouchable, *zulaal*—the cool, clear water of paradise, in which I shall bathe when my work is done. Yet she's already promised: that surely is the meaning of Fadil's words. All of a sudden I feel tears welling within me. I want to lie on the floor and give way to my grief. I catch sight of Fareed, commanding me with his immovable frown. I sit down and swallow my passion, and it burns in my throat like whisky.

Grandfather Anwar has begun to speak. Soon, he says, his grandson Qasim would arrive and we could eat our meal. Qasim is to bring the Gift, and he would show me how to use it. Until then it is best to speak of other things. He describes the days at the end of the war, during the British occupation, when he was a student in Baghdad. He joined a society of intellectuals called *jamaa'at al-waqt al-Da'i*—the society of wasted time! I tell him I have belonged to that club all my life, and today I am offering my resignation. And all at once I am happy again, recalling Halima's smile and knowing that it was meant only for me. Whatever happens, she will be mine: we shall find a way. I look up and laugh at Anwar's story, although it has become so involved I can't follow it.

The door opens and a young man in jeans walks softly across to us, places a plastic hold-all on the carpet, and shakes hands in silence. He has his sister's warm, dark eyes and her oval face, but he doesn't smile. His manner is withdrawn and enigmatic.

He sits down and begins to talk about the match: he just can't believe that Hopkins could have flunked that final penalty. He had been betting on victory: a draw means twenty quid lost, and he is even wondering whether he should go with Arsenal now. But then, it's early days. Maybe Spurs will pick up over the summer.

Then I have an idea. I ask them if I could change. She'll know I am wearing the T-shirt for her. Qasim takes me out into the hallway and points to a door on the landing. It is the dark side of the house, and from the bathroom window I have a view over gardens, most of them full of junk: fridges, telly sets, the frames of gutted motorbikes. The bathroom is real kitsch: more turquoise (basins this time), Aladdin lamps in copper alloy, pink carpets and a fluffy lambs-wool cover on the toilet. But there are only man-things round the sink: razors, shaving soap, after-shave. I am glad of that. I didn't want to think of her sharing a bathroom with the men. I get into the jeans and the T-shirt, and stand in front of the mirror: fantastic!

Nobody makes any remark when I re-enter the living room. In fact, they hardly seem to notice me. Anwar is still talking about Baghdad, saying what a fantastic education he got there—the old British curriculum, German, French, science too. Of course, that's all finished now, he says. Take Halima, for instance: she has got to GCSE in French, but can't speak a word of it, and when they took her away from school two years ago it was because of a thing called Health Education which was all about, well, about things girls shouldn't know. I go hot and cold, and my fists are clenching and unclenching in my pockets. Fareed is nodding agreement, and Qasim just sits on the divan, with a cold, concentrated stare that suggests he has heard his granddad banging on like this for far too long.

But then Zeynab pokes her head round the door and everything changes. *Ghada'* is ready, and we exchange sudden greetings and smiles. Zeynab comes across and embraces me like a son, chiding me for being so thin, teasing me about the T-shirt. Qasim takes my hand and calls me brother, and Granddad lapses into a gentle smile as we go through the door to the kitchen. How good they seem, so simple with each other, so full of kindness. And there to wait on us is Halima, who looks furtively in my direction and blushes.

There's a big table in the centre of the kitchen, spread with food: labneh, hummus, kibbeh, meat-balls with tahini and piles of unleavened bread. Halima and Zeynab stand at the stove, whispering to each other as they prepare each plate. I can hardly eat, and all my thought is how not to look at *her*. Yet I do look, and a flame shoots through me, seeing that she's in the same predicament! Yes, Halima is turning her eyes in every direction except the one towards which they steal of their own accord! I try to attend to what the men are saying, but it all seems so remote, so fantastic—part of a world I have left behind. Of course I have to know how to operate the Gift; but we made these things at school, and they all worked on a single principle. I listen to Qasim's instructions and nod, but my thoughts are elsewhere.

My eyes roam the kitchen. This is her space, the space she shares with Zeynab. Every object speaks of love, family and joy: the gilded coffee cups on their polished tray; the wooden bread bowl and the plastic-topped sideboard beneath it; the ornamental fruit-crusher just like the one brought from back home by Ami, may the peace and blessing of Allah be upon her. And beyond the long window the sunlight full of promise.

All that Fareed has planned for me is good, since it comes from here. And I'll earn the right to Halima regardless of her father's schemes. Fadil is pushing dishes in my direction, making gestures with his open hand. This and all his house will be mine.

You have to give it to Fareed. He can hold his own in any conversation. I've heard him take the floor on every subject that people talk about: pop-stars, football, all the soaps on telly, politics, even serious things like maths and bridge-building. Now he's telling Granddad Anwar about his days in Birmingham, studying engineering at the University, doing night school in Business Studies, helping out in his uncle's kebab house, saving every penny. No Wasted Time Club for Fareed: and he even managed to relax, go dancing, get himself a girlfriend, play football on Saturdays.

Anwar listens, stroking his goatee beard and sceptically cocking his head. Education, he says, means books, books, and more books. In Baghdad, they read the classics in Farsi, in Arabic, in English. They were aiming to be citizens of the world. Fareed laughs at that. Education, he retorts, means diagrams, flow charts, figures, facts. And the proof of it is there in Fareed, with three businesses to his name, a smart house in Kensington, and not yet thirty-five. Not that he mentions his successes. That's not Fareed's style. No, it's all said in a spirit of kindness, and if Anwar regrets his poverty—and all of a sudden I saw that it is poverty surrounding us, that kitsch is merely wealth imagined, that the *ghada'* is the best the family can do and probably a whole week's budget—it is not Fareed who reminds him of it but he himself, with those memories of a place to which he will never return and from which he has escaped with only useless knowledge. A shadow passes across Anwar's features, and he looks sadly at his son. It's clear that Fadil is an invalid. Once or twice he has got up from the table and gone out with slow shuffling steps, his hands held slightly to each side as though supporting himself on an imaginary Zimmer frame. I picture him sitting about all day in a state of depression, listening to that awful music from back home, or watching the telly in the heat of the day. Zeynab's smiles and embraces are not a sign of happiness at all, but a policy, a way of coping with the fact that they are not coping.

I am overcome with pity. Here and now I resolve to help these people. I will work for Fareed in textiles or road-building. Maybe the recording business since he has a line there too. And when things are right, I could buy a big house in a smart suburb, Richmond—I have always liked Richmond—or maybe Greenwich. Halima's family could come to live with us there. Abba too would come, of course. Everything within our walls will be bathed in kindness as by the light of the sun. Fantastic! I lose track of the conversation. I want to jump up and pace outside, to wait there for Halima who will come to fetch me. I am rehearsing what I shall say to her. How marvellous it will sound, spoken in that concrete yard, with all the signs of poverty around us, and our two young faces feeding on each other's hope!

Suddenly Fareed is standing behind my chair, his hand on my shoulder. I have no idea how he got there, or how it is that Qasim, too, is standing next to him. Anwar and Fadil are muttering somewhere out of sight, and there's no sign of the women. The meal is over, and a *finjan* of un-drunk coffee stands on the table.

"O.K.," I say, "let's go."

There are only the three of us in the living room. I can't

attend to their words, and besides, I know exactly what's expected. Only the size of the Gift surprises me—you could carry it in a pocket. Not like the clumsy boxes that Ginger Wilcox used to make at school. This is a real professional job; but then, what would you expect with Fareed in charge? He keeps frowning at me, because my mind is wandering.

"Fine," I say at last. "I know all this. Just trust me."

Fareed responds with a long cool look, and then hands me the bag. I push in the clothes I am carrying, and replace it on the floor.

"Excuse me a moment."

I rush from the room. Fareed and Qasim stare after me, but make no attempt to follow. Yes, she is standing there in the hallway. She beckons to the back door. We are in the garden, in the shadow of the house; a few bushes push up through the gravel. An old tin shed divides the garden from the yard next door. Not to touch her, not to look at her wrongly, not to let anything be spoiled. She is smiling though, and I can't help stealing a glance at her eyes.

"That's a cool T-shirt," she says. She speaks English, carving a little space outside the family.

"You like it?"

"Oasis: cool."

"You listen much?"

"When I can: my friend Aysha has everything."

"Halima..."

She turns, looks at me, and takes a step away.

"I really wanted to talk to you," she says.

"Yes," is all I can manage.

"Just to say I think you're great!"

She says it in a whisper, but the whole world seems to shake from the force of it. Then she runs into the house, not waiting for my reply. I go after her. There she is in the hallway, Zeynab's arms around her like a *mandil*, both of them smiling. Qasim puts the hold-all in my hand and Fareed comes with me to the door. He points the way to the station: I am on my own now.

"Don't worry," he says. "God is with you."

The cat's still there on the gatepost. We box together for a bit, and I sing 'Street Fighting Man'. The sun is warm on my neck and arms, and the cat and I are alone. I think of going back to the house, asking for Halima, making everything plain between us. But isn't it plain already? A little breeze comes playing towards me, shaking blossom from the cherry trees, ruffling the fur on the back of the cat. Suddenly it jumps from the post, arches itself angrily and dashes away.

I get lost, straying into a street of factories and repair shops. There's a little patch of grass with a bench on which a frail-looking man is sitting. He has a thermos flask in a canvas bag, a folded copy of *The Mirror*, and a walking stick that he has propped against the arm of the bench. A few pigeons have assembled in front of him, waiting for scraps of his lunch. He wears a tattered blue pullover above his trousers, and his head is almost bald. I want to go up to him, put my arm around him, tell him of my happiness, make the world smile for him as it smiles for me. Then he turns quite suddenly, and looks at me with a suspicious scowl. I ask him the way to the station. He answers with a shrug, like he is ridding himself of an unpleasant thought.

Further down the street I catch up with a young mother pushing a pram. She points me back the way I have come, and wishes me luck. I tickle the baby's soft cheek and go away laughing. How pleasant the sun is, and the wild flowers along the embankment! Soon I am climbing the steps to the platform, the bag in one hand, gripping the wooden rail with the other. There's a warm breeze blowing off the shingles, and a slight smell of engine oil. It reminds me of Abba's tools, and I am filled with love for him. That house in Richmond—or Greenwich—will repay him for everything. I amuse myself on the platform, furnishing the house in my imagination, designing a sitting room for Halima, a workshop for Abba, and a quiet study somewhere for old Anwar to lose himself in books.

Then I remember. What's the time? Four o'clock, late by half an hour. I look around me: nobody stands on the inbound platform apart from me and an old woman with a wheelie bag. Should I approach her? Probably not. Fareed said the trains run every twenty minutes; Sally won't leave the flat until half past six. All the same, I begin to get nervous. What if I don't make it? I stand to lose Halima, marriage, the house in Richmond, the chance I long for and which has never come my way before, to put everything right with Abba and with Ami too, and to show them my love. I stamp my feet impatiently. Maybe there has been an accident on the line, a strike, a power-failure. Then the rail begins to vibrate from the approaching train: the whole world is vibrating with it, and I can hardly control my trembling as I step aboard.

I find an empty place, pick up the paper that someone has left on the seat opposite and bury my head in it. It is an article about rock-climbing; it describes the writer clinging to the cliff face as the colleague above him falls into space, to swing above the void on the writer's harness. It is really gripping, and for a moment I am so lost in the story that I don't notice the ticket inspector looking down through bulbous lenses at the top of my head.

I search for a ticket. Then I remember it was Fareed who paid for us, and who is still holding the returns. What a stupid oversight! I have no money, only my pass for the tube. I try to explain everything, how I got on at a station whose name I don't remember, after visiting friends whose address I have never known, now travelling home without money to a place I would rather not disclose. I keep the discussion going for a while, but the sweat is gathering on my brow. Disaster is travelling towards us down the tube of time. We stop at a station, and I contemplate a dash for the platform. And maybe that would be best—simply to run as I have always run to Abba's workshop, to abandon everything and to cry once again in his arms. Except that Abba is working in Leeds, and I am on my own.

Then, rummaging in my back pocket, I come across a ten-pound note pressed against the lining. Sally gave me the money to buy supper since she'll be coming back late. For some reason, I have forgotten all about it. After I have paid the fare, only three pounds fifty remains—not enough for supper, but enough for a couple of drinks. The conductor nods contemptuously as he hands me the ticket, and I want to say "woe to the unbelievers, for the day that they are promised."

I cheer up though, because Halima is waiting for me and will surely send me a sign. By the time I am out of the tube and turning the corner towards Sally's flat, I am singing "Be Here Now" and smiling at the sun as it sets behind the chimneys on St Michael's Street.

Sally is working on the agenda for her meeting. I put down the bag in the corridor and say hello. She doesn't reply, but when I turn on the TV she looks up and says "I thought you were out for the day."

"I was. Only I'm back."

Sometimes Sally can make you feel really unwanted.

"Where did you go?"

"Friends," I say. There's this amazing thing on the news—a train crash in Turkey, with carriages hanging over a precipice and one of them upside down in the river below. The carriages have old-fashioned wooden doors with brass handles, and one of them is open with a body hanging out. I am trying to catch what the announcer is saying, but Sally says to switch the thing off and talk to her like she existed at least. This isn't the kind of trouble I want, so I do as I'm told.

Sally has beautiful hair: long, fair, with golden lights and a straw-coloured fringe across her brow. Without it, her face would look too broad and flat, on account of a snub nose and eyes that drift off to either side of it. But the hair makes her look great: the brainy librarian when dressed, Lady Godiva with her clothes off. She likes you to stroke her hair, which is how we got together, when I tried those evening classes in philosophy and she was the girl in front. Not that we have ever been together, except for the sex and her feeding me when Abba is working up in Leeds. And anyway, she has this boyfriend who got her involved in the Anglo-Jewish thing, which was what made me remember my promise to Ami.

So I switch off the telly—right in the middle of a great shot of the upside-down carriage in the torrent—and go across to stroke her hair. She looks up at me with half a smile, and starts gathering her papers. When she has gone, I can sit down here and write the letter to Halima—nothing florid or romantic or perfumed, but plain speech from the heart. Not marriage-broker Arabic, but ordinary English between boy and girl. Then I remember I hadn't got her address. I'll have to ask Fareed for it, and maybe Fareed wouldn't want to be in touch just yet, and wouldn't give the address in any case. And I find myself staring into the tunnel down which disaster is approaching, seeing shapeless things that move and grow and rearrange themselves in the dark.

"Where did you get that moronic T-shirt?" Sally asks.

I'm glad she doesn't like it.

"You shouldn't have got involved in this thing," I say.

She sighs loudly.

"I mean, you don't have to be there tonight. We could go out for a pizza."

"Look Yusuf, I'm a grown woman, who makes choices and who tries to live by them."

"But why choose to be a Jew?"

Because that is how it seems to me.

"Yusuf, I sometimes think you're a racist."

She puts the papers in her brief-case and goes angrily to the bathroom. It's only a moment's work, to take the Gift from the hold-all, twist down the top, and hide it in her papers. She's still looking angry when she comes back. Her boyfriend is an American Jew called Milton—Milt for short. He's married, with kids, and spends his life commuting back and forth between London and Chicago. I know this because she told me one day, after a bottle of wine, when she was missing him. Sally may be a grown woman, but she can make really stupid choices. But I suppose it's not my business, and besides she's hurrying away now, snatching up the briefcase and saying she has left it all so late she would have to get a taxi. At the door she turns and looks at me. Something cold runs through me like a knife.

"Don't go," I say.

Then she smiles, blows me a kiss, and says "you fool." In a second she is down the stairs and in the street, running away from me.

The sun has almost set, and long shadows lie across the pavement. I wander around Sally's neighbourhood. I have a beer in the Three Feathers, and then a whisky in the Crown and Anchor. I think of Halima, and I am sad that Abba is away in Leeds, staying in that cheap hotel where he can never be reached. I ring Fareed from a call box but his mobile is switched off. Then I decide to go to the Union Meeting Rooms.

The place is cordoned off, police barring the entrance. I stand across the road in a kind of dream. The evening is getting chilly, and I still have nothing on save the jeans and the T-shirt. I remember Jenny and look in my pockets for her phone number. It's no longer there. For some reason this makes me feel really lonely.

I go back to Sally's flat. I am hungry now, but I can't find anything in the fridge save a few tomatoes and a piece of stale cheese. The ten o'clock news is all about a taxi that has exploded in Central London. The occupants—the driver and an unidentified female—were killed. A few bystanders injured by flying debris, one of them seriously.

I watch for a while, and then switch channels, hoping for the rail crash in Turkey. But now I remember: I am to meet up with Fareed at ten thirty in Trafalgar Square. I arrive there breathless at ten thirty-five, still in my Oasis T-shirt. Now it's really cold, and I walk up and down between the waterless pools shivering and clutching my arms across my chest. After five minutes I discover Fareed walking at my side. How long he has been there I don't know. He is dressed very smartly, in a dark suit and tie, and his face is gathered in a frown.

"I fucked it up, didn't I?"

"Look Yusuf," he says, "you were supposed to wait until she was at the door. I told you it was primed for twenty minutes."

I nod, though I have no such recollection.

"They're all going to think badly of me, aren't they?"

"When we get to the corner," he says, ignoring me, "I shall give you an envelope. Use the money to get away, O.K.? And don't try to be in touch."

"But Fareed..."

My heart sinks in dismay. He is my hero, my commander. Without him I'm lost.

"I shall be abroad, in any case," he went on. "We are leaving tomorrow."

"We?"

"I mean, me and Halima."

I continue to walk briskly, although my heart is dead.

"And her family?" I manage at last.

He shrugs.

"They'll cope. After their fashion."

We're at the corner. He slips me the envelope and walks on without a word.

Veronica

THEY WERE SITTING BESIDE THE POOL, the steam rising above their knees, and in each of their faces was a light of hilarity and adventure. The small man had taken some bananas from the basket on his knee and, peeling them one by one, he handed the glistening sticks to his companions, laughing from his large brown eyes as they reached out to grasp them. One of the girls said "yuk!" in a childish voice, and the man leaned across to whisper in her ear. She screamed and fell backwards into the pool, her brown legs scissoring as she went. The man gave a bark of satisfaction, and closed his mouth with a banana.

Veronica watched as the fruit disappeared between his large red lips and resolved itself into mounds of cheek-flesh. The man was her new uncle, and she didn't like him. She didn't like him at all, and had made up her mind to tell mother at the first opportunity, even though mother would be cross. Uncle Gerald would have gone sooner if Veronica had said how much she hated him. And that's what she intended to do with Simon. There was no point in waiting when you were sure. Just look at the way he was chewing on that banana, how amusing he thought he was, and all that swank when he couldn't be more than five foot six on the outside.

It was due to Simon that the pool was so warm. He had turned up the thermostat, giggling like a naughty boy, as Aunt Jerry and the twins scampered at his heels thinking what a laugh he was. Now the water was steaming and drops of condensation were forming on the steel girders under the roof. One of them fell on to Veronica's neck. It was cold and unpleasant and she pulled her T-shirt across to absorb it. Both the twins were in the water now, Anna splashing and blowing spray from her puffed-up face, Julie standing in the shallow end, looking at her mother and Simon. Simon's friend was laughing too. He was eighteen and good-looking, with long black eyelashes and almond eyes like the Italian waiter in the Swan Hotel. His name was Tony, and he was still at school. Veronica planned to leave school in three years time when she was sixteen. She would go a long way from Ingleton Court, maybe even as far as Burston, to work in the hairdresser's there and stay in a bed and breakfast. Then, when she had enough money, she would go to Paris, and be the mistress of a famous man. Quite which famous man was not yet decided. She supposed there would have to be negotiations first.

Veronica was disappointed in Julie. When the twins came for their summer holidays, she and Julie would spend their days together, and now that mother had bought the pony—the first they'd had since poor Clover died—they were to take it in turns to ride. But Julie, who was nearly fifteen, had become interested in boys. This fatal weakness, which had nothing in common with Veronica's mature decision to become a mistress since it was based in no strategy for social advancement or for advancement of any kind, had damaged their friendship irreparably. No sooner did a boy appear on the scene—and he did not have to be as good-looking as Tony—than Julie would enter another and more foolish frame of mind. Her voice would rise in pitch and volume, her remarks would become more pointed and public, her gestures would lose their hesitation, and all the sweet obedience of her childhood ways would vanish. Veronica tried hard to forgive her, to go on loving her, to be her true companion. But Julie failed to notice Veronica's efforts, and the distance between the real and the remembered Julie grew as water grows between a cast-off boat and its mooring.

Matters had come to a head with Tony. Simon had brought him to stay a week ago, and they had all been excited—Aunt Jerry, the twins, Nanny Draper and even Muddy the terrier who understood that at any moment the world was going to change. Mother had told them at supper time, saying Tony was a special boy who had lost his parents when very little but was so clever that Uncle Simon had sort of adopted him, had paid for his schooling, and was coaching him for Oxford. Uncle Simon, Mother said, was like that, a man who did not wait for others to do good, but stepped in and took charge of it himself. She hoped that the girls would be as lucky as Tony was, since everyone needs a benefactor, especially those who have no father to look after them. Simon had smiled through this speech, making tut-tut noises of a self-deprecating kind, which made Veronica's flesh creep. She had tried to catch Julie's eye, so that she could discreetly raise her eyebrows with a "What a phony!" look. But Julie was too excited to notice, and was pumping Mother with questions about Tony's age, interests, height, colouring and favourite pop group.

Veronica's fears were realized. When the boy arrived next day, driven from the station in the bright red Aston Martin that was Simon's title to devotion, he began a systematic conquest of the women. Charm was his policy; he paid court to Mother, commenting favourably on the summer dress which Veronica deplored since it was cut so low and showed half of Mother's sun-tanned bust, besides being of a canary yellow colour that suited no one over thirty. He carried things to and fro, volunteered for little jobs like serving drinks or laying the table—jobs that required no great effort but which all the same put him on display as a conscientious guest of the family. He helped Aunt Jerry with the shopping, showed her how to work the video camera, and taught the twins to play "Chop-Sticks" on the piano. He was polite to Nanny Draper, and pretended to understand her when she whispered on about the Bible. And he was so fascinated by Muddy and the pony that you would have honestly suspected he had never met an animal before. In short, he was an invincible intruder, and easily the match in that department for Simon, who encouraged him constantly with silent smiles. Nothing had been said about the length of Tony's stay, and within a week Veronica felt so estranged from the proceedings that she was considering advancing her departure.

The only problem was that she did not think she was ready to be a mistress just yet, besides having serious doubts about the legality of the thing, even in France.

They were out of the pool now, and Simon was pulling Aunt Jerry by the wrist and leading her out on to the lawn with a loping ape-like dance. She laughed at his buffoonery, while Tony, meticulous in his little courtesies, handed a pair of towels to the twins and ushered them after their mother. Almost forgetting, he stopped in his tracks and turned to Veronica.

"Coming?" he asked with a smile.

She made no answer.

"See you outside, then."

He turned and walked quietly after the twins, his bare back swaying on his polished legs. After a while Veronica got up from her chair and went to the glass doors of the veranda. They were on the lawn now, Simon cavorting with Aunt Jerry, and the twins running in circles around them. She wondered why Tony stood apart, his face serious and frowning, as though lost in thought. Thought was not a common attribute of boys as she had known them. And thought had been banished from the house by Simon, whose squeaks and giggles had reduced everyone to happy animals, rushing around and against one another like a pack of excited puppies. How wearisome it had all become, and how interminable.

She had asked Mother what Simon did.

"It's difficult to explain," she replied with that queer look of hers which meant ask no questions and you'll hear no lies. Then she nodded to a book that was lying on the coffee table. "That's something he wrote there, so you can see for yourself."

But she said it in a non-committal way, as though to imply

that Simon was far more important than a mere author—certainly more important than *The Wines of Tuscany* by Simon Goldcastle. Veronica glanced at the book. It was illustrated with crude line-drawings of Tuscan farms and cypress trees, and every page was headed with the name of a village, and a paragraph of statistics about hectares, hectolitres and grape varietals. It was the kind of book that anyone could put together from official reports, with the aid of a leisurely holiday. Mother and Simon had been to Tuscany in the spring, just after he had been introduced as her newest uncle.

"Surely he can't make a living from books like this," Veronica said.

"Of course not. That's just the icing on the cake."

A dull cake was Veronica's thought. But she dropped the subject, not wanting to give the impression that her interest in Simon went further than a passing curiosity. The deeper the interest, the more durable the fact.

Watching Simon's gambols, she was struck by the idea that he would not have told the truth about his occupation in any case. Just how she arrived at this idea she did not know. But it came upon her so forcefully that she could not dismiss it. And then—why not?—it would be interesting to unmask him. She went with a new and more cheerful outlook through the veranda doors.

Tony was still standing apart from the fun, in the shade of the tulip tree at the edge of the lawn. He smiled at her as she passed. She made a grimace at him, and then changed the grimace to a half-smile.

"When's your mother back?" he asked.

She shrugged her shoulders.

"In time for lunch."

She tried not to look at him, but his smile remained and held her eyes. Once, years ago, a man had smiled at her like that. It was in the supermarket where she had gone shopping with Nanny Draper. He had stood by the ice-box, with an empty trolley in front of him, dressed in a bright yellow windproof. He was young, with smooth film-star looks like Tony. He had offered to buy her an ice-cream. Nanny Draper had walked up behind her quickly, taken her hand, and hurried her unspeaking away.

"Your mother is very good," he said suddenly. "The way she always cooks for us, and the way—I mean, she doesn't seem to mind us being here."

"Oh," said Veronica, "she wouldn't show it, even if she did mind."

He looked puzzled.

"Do you think she does mind then?"

She wondered whether this question had ever occurred to him before.

"Oh well, I suppose not. All things considered."

"What things?"

"Simon, for one thing."

He laughed.

"Oh, I know he is someone special for your mother."

Veronica sensed the raw, red feeling as it came rushing up through her gorge and briefly boiled in her throat before escaping with a hiss into the atmosphere. She watched it fly aloft, flapping angrily, a great bird now, a bird of prey circling high above them, a dwindling dot, now fixed like a star with its eye on the unsuspecting Simon.

"He's not specially special," she said quietly. "Not so special as you think."

"No, I don't suppose he is," Tony said hurriedly, with an embarrassed look. He had taken something from the pocket of his shorts, and held it out to her. It was a shiny metallic cylinder.

"What is it?" she asked.

"A present. I've been meaning to give it to you all morning, only I didn't want the others to see."

Veronica recoiled. The thought of something between her and Tony, which the others should not see, filled her with distaste. She shook her head.

"Please take it," he said. "It will help you."

"Help me what?"

"Help you understand."

There was a strange beseeching light in his eyes. She tried for a moment to hold out against it. Then slowly she extended her hand. The object that he placed in it was warm with body heat, smooth and heavy like an ingot.

"It's a sculpture," he said. "And there's another one inside."

In her hand lay a fish of yellow metal, which stared up at her with a blue glass eye. The body was cylindrical, with a joint running behind the fins. He took it from her and unscrewed the tail. And when he shook the fish another object slid from it into the palm of his hand. Veronica tried not to look at it.

"You see? It's a man who was eaten."

The figure was crouching with its chin pressed to its knees. It had a curious melancholy expression on its face, which seemed full of knowledge.

"It must be very valuable," she said. "You shouldn't give it away."

He put the man back into the fish and screwed it together. "But I want you to have it," he said. "It'll help you understand."

"Understand what?"

He was looking away from her to the group on the lawn, who had fallen silent. His face was troubled.

"What's been happening here. I mean with me and your mother and Simon."

Veronica thought for a moment.

"Where did you get it?"

"I found it. One day, when I was out with Simon. We were visiting some people in a big house. Down near Southampton."

She wondered why Tony was telling her this, and the suspicion formed in her mind that he had stolen the little sculpture, and was trying to implicate her in the theft. Tony came with Simon, and Simon was bad. Therefore Tony was probably bad too. Veronica shook her head.

"I don't want it," she said.

He looked thoughtful for moment.

"O.K. Then I'll keep it for you."

"Why, if I don't want it?"

He did not answer, but returned the fish to his pocket, and walked slowly away towards the group on the lawn. Aunt Jerry threw the ball in his direction, and he ran to catch it. How stupid they were. And look at mother, just arrived, all flustered with her shopping bags, and coming straight into the garden. Veronica was ashamed for her, and turned her back on the scene as Simon, who was dancing on one leg, hopped in Mother's direction for his good morning kiss.

That afternoon they went on a picnic to Abbotsford. Mother,

Muddy and the children travelled in the Land Rover, Aunt Jerry following in the Aston Martin with Simon and Tony. Julie talked all the way about Tony. She knew his favourite colour, football team, pop group and film star. She knew where he went for his holidays, what his parents had done and what they died of. She knew his address and telephone number when he wasn't with Uncle Simon. And she knew the names of the other boys in his dormitory, all of whom were orphans like himself. During the term, he was at boarding school, and Julie knew the names of the masters, which ones were cool and which ones chronic. Veronica listened in silence, while Anna, who had no time for anyone save Muddy, pressed the terrier's face against the window, and described for its benefit the fleeting scene beyond.

Mother didn't look too happy. She frowned as she drove. Her lips were pursed and the wrinkles gathered in a fan at the bridge of her nose. Something must have happened with Simon, who normally insisted that they all clamber together into the Land Rover, with Aunt Jerry driving, Veronica next to her, and the rest crowded at the back, Simon pressed between Mother and Tony.

"Have you done?" she said after a while to Julie.

"Done what?"

"Selling us Tony."

Julie pouted and said she wasn't trying to sell anyone, just relaying the news. Then they were all silent until the car stopped at the edge of the woods above Abbotsford. Mother sat at the wheel, waiting for the Aston Martin to pull up behind them. Something was wrong, however, for it did not arrive. After a minute or two Mother got out, and they followed. The long road from the vale unwound before them. They could see nothing on it save a slowly moving tractor, which turned off suddenly into a field. Veronica thought about the fish with the man inside. Why had Tony wanted to give it to her? Then suddenly she had an idea.

"I expect they've gone back home," she said.

"Gone back home? Why should they do that?"

Mother looked at her as though it were none of Veronica's business what Simon and Tony were up to.

"To case the joint."

Veronica said it with a slight American accent, so as to make it sound more dramatic and final. Muddy had begun to bark at the window, hoping to be let out.

"And you think Aunt Jerry is casing the joint too?"

"Oh no," said Veronica. "She's their alibi."

Mother swallowed slightly, her throat moving up and down. "I'm listening," she said.

"Tony's got this fantastic little fish with a man inside," said Julie suddenly. "It's amazing. You unscrew the fish and out pops the man."

"I mean," said Veronica, "'they can get lost somewhere, and one of them double back to the house without Aunt Jerry ever thinking that he isn't just as lost as she is."

"Did you know you have a wicked imagination?"

"Yes," Veronica replied, and she felt tense and defiant inside.

"I mean, did you realize that whenever anything good happens in my life you try to spoil it?"

Mother's cheeks had begun to tremble. Veronica and her mother were standing in the air outside. White wind-driven clouds scudded across the hillsides, their shadows moving in the steel-grey grass like ruffling hands. The twins got out too, and went shrieking after Muddy as he ran in the wood. The Aston

Martin appeared around the corner in the valley. It was travelling very slowly and jerkily. It seemed strangely out of place in this landscape, like a doodle on a precious painting. Mother was still, too upset to speak. Veronica recalled her father, his smell of tobacco, and the golden fob-watch which used to dangle from his pocket above her as he bent to kiss her goodnight. She did not blame him for dying, but she regretted that he had given no instructions as to how to live thereafter.

The Aston Martin came up beside them and lurched to a halt. Aunt Jerry was at the wheel, with Tony beside her. They looked very serious, like refugees.

"Hi," said Veronica and looked away. Mother was beside her now, anxiously flapping her hands.

"Where's Simon?" she cried. "Has something happened? What's the matter?"

There was a silence as Aunt Jerry and Tony looked at each other.

"He went off on his own," said Aunt Jerry in a solemn voice.

"Where?" asked Mother. "I mean, where did he leave?"

"Just back there, at the bottom of the wood. We wanted to go with him. But he said no, we should go on."

"What the hell is he playing at?" asked Mother.

Veronica looked away. How distressing it was—the phoniness, the stupidity. Simon would be back at the house by now, sorting through their possessions. She didn't mind losing them. On the contrary, most of them gave her the creeps, since they reminded her of Father. The house and furniture were his. And nothing in the drawing room had been changed since the day he died. That's why Mother never went there.

"He said there was somewhere he wanted to visit," Tony

said, "somewhere special."

Veronica heard this with an inner sarcastic smile. She looked at Mother.

"Well then," Mother said at last, "I expect he'll join us."

"But how will he find us?" Veronica asked.

"Maybe he knows the way."

It was Tony who spoke, with a strange quiet tone as though making a decision.

"I'm hungry," said Anna. Aunt Jerry clambered from the Aston Martin. The driver's seat was so low against the chassis that she had to push with her buttocks while clinging to the frame of the door. Tony jumped out nimbly on the other side and came round to help her. Veronica decided that she had never really liked Aunt Jerry, except as Julie's mother, which made her inevitable. Mother began to unload the folding chairs, a blanket, and a plastic bottle of sun-cream. She advanced towards Veronica, the bottle extended, a tense expression on her face. Veronica ducked away.

"No, Mother. I don't need it."

"Reason not the need," said Mother angrily.

"I think I must look for Simon," said Tony, still speaking softly and to no one in particular.

"You don't know this wood," said Mother, "you'll get lost." Veronica had a sudden inspiration.

"I'll go with him," she offered, and out of the corner of her eye she caught a glimpse of Julie, who pursed her lips in a petulant way. It was typical of Julie to see her own motives in everyone. It hadn't crossed her mind that Tony and Simon were criminals and that someone must keep an eye on them.

But you could see that it had crossed Mother's mind, for

she lowered the arm with the sun-cream bottle, looked unsurely into Veronica's eyes and said, "OK. Take Muddy with you."

Veronica went on ahead. The smooth trunks of beech trees patrolled the wood, regular as colonnades, raising a great vault of branches above them. Their canopy of silver-green leaves fluttered in the afternoon breeze, scattering shards of light through the upper air. Once or twice, a squirrel scampered down from the sunlight and hung upside down to observe them with trembling nose, its button eyes like phials of light in the woodland gloom. Muddy ran through the bracken, occasionally yelping at a smell, but always swerving back to them, pausing on the track ahead before jumping again into the undergrowth. Tony caught up with her.

"I suppose you don't like me," he said.

"Oh," she replied, with a non-committal shrug. She wondered why the people Mother brought into her life wanted her to like them. She didn't want to be liked. She had other plans.

"I mean," he continued, "you always seem so—so disgruntled."

"Why should I be gruntled?"

Tony didn't reply, and for a while there was only the sound of their feet in the bracken, and the occasional muffled yelp from Muddy as he explored the undergrowth ahead. Whatever Tony and Simon were planning, she thought, it was for the long term. Not a theft but a take-over.

"Anyway," he said at last, "I like you. Shall I tell you why?"

She shrugged her shoulders again. Whatever he said wasn't going to change her view of him. He was a dummy, a puppet, a pretence.

"I like you because you see through things. You see what's trapped inside."

Veronica thought about this as she watched a pheasant that Muddy had startled, and which took off through the branches with a squawk and a clatter of wings. She couldn't imagine anything trapped inside Tony.

"Where do you think Simon went?" she asked. It seemed like the most effective way to change the subject. But something in Tony's response caused her involuntarily to look round at him. His eyes were tearful and his mouth trembled slightly.

"He was very upset," he said.

"Oh."

"Yes, he knows you see through him."

"Really?"

"It's like the thing I wanted to give you: the little man inside the fish. I know the little man. And I see the silly fish, splashing and buffooning and making such a fool of itself. And I feel ashamed of him, and ashamed for being part of him. But I have to play the game. I know I shouldn't say this."

Veronica listened in astonishment.

"What game?" she asked. They had arrived at a little clearing, where there had been a cottage of stone. Two of the walls still stood, visible through the choking screen of brambles. Veronica thought of the life that these walls had sheltered and which had now vanished from the world. She felt a peculiar sensation, as though falling unhindered into the past. And suddenly she remembered something—something that promised to explain Simon, Tony, Mother, everything.

"I call it hide and seek," said Tony, who seemed calmer now. "Hiding what you are, and seeking what isn't yours."

"You mean stealing things?"

"You could call it stealing. Sometimes it feels like that."

Tony looked at her, and his look seemed humble and beseeching. If he were really a thief, she reflected, he would not confess the fact so easily.

"Only of course it isn't literally stealing," he went on, "when the victim consents. You see Simon is like me—he has got nothing of his own."

Veronica gave a scornful shake of the head.

"He's got an Aston Martin."

"I'm not talking about toys, Veronica."

She didn't like him using her name and walked on in silence. It was shortly before Father died: she must have been seven, maybe just eight. They were riding at the edge of the meadow, she on Clover, he on the big black hunter called Jim. It had been a difficult morning, Father just back from the city, tetchy and belligerent, Veronica frightened of the pony and out of sorts because she had quarrelled with Nanny Draper, probably about nothing, or maybe about borrowing Mother's makeup. Jim had begun to canter and then took the bit between his teeth which got Clover going too and soon the animals were racing out of control through the gate and on to the bridleway below the wood. Someone was walking in front of them: a small bald man with a loping gait who seemed lost in thought. Father was crying out to him, but the man seemed not to hear. The bridleway was narrow, hemmed in on both sides by tall hedges of blackthorn. There seemed to be no way that the man could save himself. Veronica screamed and the man turned.

He stared at her from large brown eyes and then threw out his hands as though to ward them off; in an instant the horses were over him, thundering on towards the old stone cottage by the wood. Later, when they had wrestled the horses to walking pace, Veronica looked back down the bridleway. The man stood at the place where they had galloped over him, staring into the void. Veronica wanted to go back and apologize, but her father, whose face was livid with anger, forbad it with a snort. They rode on past the cottage.

It was the man on the bridleway that Veronica had suddenly remembered, recalling the ghost-pale face and wide brown eyes in which she had seen both terror and sadness. And now she could put a name to that face, and the name was Simon. A queer feeling of triumph came over her.

"So what is it you and Simon haven't got?" she asked, slowing a little so that Tony could come up beside her. "Oh, I know what *you* haven't got, and that's parents. But when you're Simon's age you don't need parents anyway."

"No," said Tony, "but you need the thing that parents give you. You need a home."

"But you can't go around stealing other people's homes. I mean, you can steal their furniture, their houses even. But that's not the same."

"You've noticed then."

Tony spoke sadly. Veronica's thoughts were racing now. Maybe Tony was an ally. Oh, he obeyed Simon's instructions; he charmed the ladies and was a foil to Simon's saintliness-my-foot. But he didn't like what was happening any more than she did.

"Can't Simon be your home? I mean, can't he adopt you?"

"He'd have to be married. And I wouldn't like his wife."

"So what's the solution?"

"There isn't one. Only Veronica..."

Muddy barked loudly and furiously at something just out

of sight. They were approaching the edge of the wood now, and the sunlight on the meadow was visible through the trees. Muddy went suddenly quiet.

"Only what?" she asked.

"Only, you see, Simon has never settled down. He's the only thing I've got, but I can't hold on to him. He's everywhere; which means he's nowhere."

"You're wrong. He's here."

And Veronica pointed to the figure sitting on a tree-stump at the edge of the wood. The man had one hand on Muddy, who was resting on his haunches and wagging his tail in the bracken; the man's other hand was clamped to his face as though in pain. He rocked back and forth so that his bald head kept bobbing into a shaft of sunlight and out again. He knew they were watching him, Veronica concluded, which was why he was putting on this show. It occurred to her that Simon had been three weeks at Ingleton, yet they had exchanged hardly a word. She strode forward ahead of Tony.

"You've found me," Simon said, without looking round. There was a tremor in his voice, which Veronica dismissed as theatrical.

"It wasn't hard," she said. "You weren't trying to escape."

Simon sighed.

"I wish I could," he said, "I wish I could."

And slowly he lowered his hand from his face and looked round at her. She hated it when adults cried. Their faces became rag-like and soppy; the control of things, which after all was their responsibility, fled from their features; the futility of existence, the pointlessness of growing up, were blatantly displayed as in some grotesque satirical advert. And the eyes, which were designed by God to look out from their sockets like bright policemen, turned inwards, and showed you their sightless backs. The effect was particularly disgusting in a person whom you could not like, and Simon's crumpled face as it slowly turned to her caused her to shudder and look away.

"You did though, once," she said.

Tony was beside her, looking at the ground and kicking at a tuft of grass. He wore bespoke shoes that had been carefully polished. He was always immaculately presented and she wondered all of a sudden where his money came from.

Simon rose slowly to his feet.

"Sorry, Tony old chap. I was being a bit sentimental. Hope you weren't too worried."

"Oh, you know..."

"You didn't have to come back," Veronica persisted. "You could have found somewhere of your own, just like Aunt Jerry and the twins when Uncle Toby kicked her out."

Simon's face was settled now and sombre, and he looked at her gravely from his deep brown eyes.

"There is only one person I could have lived with. See over there?"

He swung round quickly and pointed to the cottage across the meadow. The new owners had put bright orange curtains in the windows, and the garden was full of junk.

"I tried to buy that place. All those years ago. When Harry Ingleton got wind of it, he stepped in and bought it for himself."

"You mean Father didn't want you here either?"

She hadn't meant to be so blunt, but she didn't regret it for he had no business referring to her father. She remembered how her parents had fought over the cottage, Mother saying that they had no need for it, that he was buying it to spite her, that he was squandering the money set aside for Veronica's education, that he was behaving like his land-crazed ancestors, who had driven all natural society from Ingleton and brooded in melancholy silence in the great cold house. And so Veronica had taken Father's side. They would restore the cottage, she said, and maybe sell it at a profit. Father died two months later and the cottage stood empty for years. Then Mother sold it to pay for Uncle Mick's swimming pool. When Mick left, the cottage was sold again. Nobody knew the people who lived there now.

Simon suddenly looked at her with a wry smile.

"After that, you see, I went away, lost touch completely. For two years I never set foot in England, except once when Tony was ill."

He spoke confidingly, undeterred by her hostile stare. She thought of the man in the fish, and wondered whether she was seeing him now. She was conscious of Tony watching her, wanting her to be other than she was.

"I was a fool," Simon went on. "Behaving as though I'd been rejected."

"It sounds like you had been," she said. Something in his tone frightened her. "Let's go," she added. "They are all waiting for us. I was only showing Tony the way."

"Nice of you, Veronica. I'm sorry I've been such a nuisance."

Simon turned, waved vaguely at the meadow, and began to intone.

"For nature, heartless, witless nature,
Will neither care nor know
What stranger's feet may find the meadow
And trespass there and go,

Nor ask amid the dews of morning
If they are mine or no...'
Tony was still scuffing the turf with dust-covered shoes.
"That's all rot, Simon," he said, not looking up.
"What's all rot?"
"Housman. Victorian drivel."
"At your age, I thought the same," Simon retorted. "The censoriousness of youth. This young lady suffers from it too."

He looked at Veronica with a forgiving smile.

"Let's go," she said again. "Young lady" made her sick. She was striding along the path, and could see the dark green mound of brambles around the ruined cottage in front of her. Tony and Simon were somewhere behind, walking side by side, not bothering to catch up with her. Once, glancing back down the path, she saw them holding hands. She had made her point; she was not going to speak to them again.

During the picnic, however, Tony addressed his remarks constantly to her. They were sitting around a spread napkin bearing marmite sandwiches and a large sticky fruitcake. Julie was angling for Tony's attention; Mother was looking frowningly at Simon who stared down at his hands; Aunt Julie and Anna were stuffing their mouths in silence, having set up their chairs by the edge of the wood. Tony was talking about pop groups. He recommended Billy Idol, who was the favourite in his year at St Cuthbert's, though there was a cheesy side to him. The Beatles and the Rolling Stones you had to admire, even though they were long in the past, because they were classics, though personally, he thought it was Elvis had the real talent. Veronica made the occasional monosyllabic response, but was so struck by Simon's defeated look that she could not attend to Tony's words. Suddenly Simon looked up and said to no one in particular:

"We'll be going back tonight, if that's OK."

"Of course it's not OK," said Mother as Julie said "Oooh!" in a disappointed voice. "What on earth has got into you?"

"Tony has some shopping to do."

Mother gave Tony an accusing look, and then walked off into the wood. Simon sat for a moment before rising with a sigh to follow her.

There was a silence, and then,

"It's always like this," said Tony, "when the buffooning stops. And of course, this place is special. I mean, your mother's special."

Veronica shrugged.

"So are you," he added. "You know that, don't you?"

Veronica made no reply but stared for a while at Muddy, who was rolling delightedly on his back, scenting himself in a patch of dust. Then Julia began to gabble away about her musical tastes, mentioning groups that Veronica had never heard of, and trying to appear super-erudite about a subject over which, in Veronica's opinion, erudition was as absurd as counting aloud to a million.

Mother looked angry when she and Simon returned. Aunt Jerry had already packed the picnic things, and they drove back as they had come, with Mother, Veronica, Muddy and the twins in the Land Rover, the rest in Simon's Aston Martin. It was only as they turned the corner into the drive of Ingleton Court that Mother broke the silence.

"Why do you hate Simon?"

"I don't hate him; I just don't want him around."

Mother pursed her lips and rammed the car into a lower gear as they went over the cattle-grid. The rattle of wheels on the iron pipes made her shout the words:

"You mean a lot to Simon, did you know that?"

"How can I mean a lot to Simon? He doesn't know who I am. He doesn't know, for instance, that I am the girl who nearly ran him down six years ago on Clover. And anyway, I don't want to mean *anything* to him, so there."

Veronica sensed the onslaught of tears—tears of rage and humiliation. So Simon cared about her! The thought was like a contamination: she wanted to run away from it, to plunge into running water, to lose herself in streams of unconsciousness. Mother parked the car at the side of the house and the twins got out. Veronica waited until they had disappeared through the kitchen door before jumping on to the gravel and running down to the lake.

Tony was already there, walking on the path. He was frowning, and the long eyelashes as he turned to her seemed to wriggle slightly under the pressure of his brow.

"Don't cry, Veronica. It isn't your fault. Simon's blown it, and now we're on the move again. The usual story."

That was fine by her, but there were troubling details that needed explaining. She kept her distance from Tony, fearing he might reach out to touch her.

"But why are we special? I mean, why does Simon have to come back here, with you in tow?"

"That's what I hoped you'd understand. Simon wanted you to be part of him, as I am."

"I'm not part of anyone," she cried.

"But that's how he sees it. He wanted to be accepted here,

to have you as a friend."

Veronica thought about this for a while.

"Why isn't Mother enough for him?"

"I leave that to your imagination."

Veronica's imagination encompassed many things, but stopped short of her mother's love-affairs. She decided to change the subject.

"Are you gay?" she asked. It was OK to be gay; even more OK to show that you accepted it.

"Isn't it obvious?"

Tony looked at her askance.

"And Simon?"

"Simon? Of course not!"

"So Simon wants actually to move in here, to settle down?"

"Well, he did want that. But only on one condition."

"And what was that?"

"That he could win you over."

'Yuk!'

Suddenly there came the sound of Mother's voice calling from the house. "Tony! Tony!" It wasn't Mother's style to shout, and the sight of her waving frantically in her hideous yellow dress filled Veronica with irritation. Mother's arms milled helplessly and the dress went up and down around her knees with a ludicrous pumping motion. She seemed like a holograph, projected on to the air of Ingleton from some unseen store of comic fictions. Tony was running towards her, and Mother came down the stairway with small hurried steps to meet him. Veronica decided on a policy of indifference. Then she heard Julie screaming.

She discovered them by the swimming pool. The twins were sobbing under the diving board, Julie pressing her fists into her mouth and Anna adopting the special rabbit posture, legs crouching, arms extended, that she kept for real emergencies. Tony, Mother and Aunt Jerry pulled at Uncle Simon's feet, which were still encased in the brown leather shoes he had worn for the picnic. His shirt had come unbuttoned and floated round his head like the wings of some heraldic creature. Simon's body smacked against the side of the pool, sending little wavelets across the bare pink flesh, and when at last they lifted his stomach on to the tiles, so that only the head still lolled in the water beneath its blue cotton canopy, the arms came suddenly straight out of the water as though giving a thumbs-up of triumph.

It was only as Veronica said thank you to the woman at the ambulance service that Mother came over to speak to her. The phone clattered as Veronica replaced it, and Mother was forced to repeat her words.

"I can't blame you," she said.

Why should Veronica be blamed for this latest piece of theatre? She regretted what had happened, but it was Simon's doing, and typical of his attention-seeking ways. Thinking about this, she became tense and defiant, and her thin young body felt as though it were bound by an iron sheath.

"Father never wanted him here," Veronica said at last.

"What do you know about that?" whispered Mother between her teeth. "What do you know about that?"

"Father..."

Veronica looked up in astonishment as her mother went white with rage.

"Don't call him that, do you hear? Don't call him that!"

It seemed for a moment that she was about to strike her daughter. And then she swung on her heels and ran.

"SO YOU'RE LEAVING FOR ITALY?" Guy was saying. "Hoping to make a come back, or a go back? Well, it's your right, and who am I to stop you? In fact, to tell the truth, I'm rather glad. A decision at last."

He was drunk, and his white face, caught in the glare of a streetlamp, swayed against the back of her mother's armchair like a puffball. His pale lips seemed hardly to move, and the sound emerged into the room as though seeping from an intercom. Mary was reminded of a puppet theatre she had seen outside the church of S Maria in Trastevere. The play was political, about a man of radical convictions in the hands of the Inquisition. At a certain point, the Grand Inquisitor's great round head appeared from behind and lolled from side to side beneath the proscenium arch, while a veiled ventriloquist made threats out of all proportion to the puny figures on the stage. She had felt a sudden urge to snatch the puppets from their strings, and tell them to stop being ridiculous.

"You can't say that you haven't yourself to blame," he went on. "I warned you a hundred times against me. What does it say in the Prayer Book? 'Hear what comfortable words our Saviour Christ saith unto all that truly turn to him.' Comfortable words, words like armchairs! You can snooze your life away in them. Well, here are some uncomfortable words, words like broken glass. I made you up with holy mascara. I encouraged you to believe that crap you were brought up in: God, Jesus, the communion of saints, faith, hope, charity, etcetera. Not because you needed it, but on the contrary, because I wanted one other person to live by the code I dishonoured. With you believing I could have a good time doubting, with you hooked on hope and charity I could get a kick out of being desperate and mean. And with you as the loyal wife weeping over your sins, I could run after other women. All this last year there you stood, prim with your secret reproaches, awaiting the end."

It was Guy's normal monologue, and Mary listened to it with only half her attention. She wondered whether the time had come to turn on the light, so that she could search for the book she had been reading, and at the same time reduce the chance that Guy would stumble and break some piece of furniture. She decided to leave the room in darkness.

"Of course, you say, it's not the infidelities you mind..."

She had never said any such thing. But let it pass.

"After all, I've never put you second. I've never been able to squeeze out of myself a fraction more of love or tenderness or decency than was on offer to you, and God knows that's little enough. Imagine what *they* felt about it—knowing that I would never disturb a single one of our arrangements in order to please *them*, knowing that my nights and days were sown up forever, never to be changed in the slightest particular, and certainly not because *they* required it. It was like having an affair with a tomb, only one in which a sepulchral voice occasionally sounded. God knows what they saw in me."

Mary had been trying to identify the time when things went wrong. Was it those hectic weeks of Guy's opera, which the critics had so cruelly slated that it had to be withdrawn after the second performance? Was it the closing of the music department at Corton College, after which he had been without an income, forced to depend on her to such an extent that it became impossible, in his eyes, to consider marriage? Was it the time, two years ago, when he had invented a clandestine lover—a teenage star, a creature from the gutter with a raucous voice, a criminal record and the face of a cherub—and declared that he was leaving with her for America: a fiction all the more poignant in that Mary, who knew the girl (she was the daughter of her cousin, Podge Wilmington) had just been told of Guy's futile attempt to seduce her by the man, a fellow writer, who had not only succeeded in that enterprise, but was at that very moment flying with her for a concert tour in Singapore? Or was it the time just six months ago and still terrible to remember, when they had stood together in the Abbey church at Cirencester, breathing its vacated air, and a crowd of indecorous schoolchildren had entered—the moment when she had realized, all of a sudden and in a suffocating panic, that her Christian faith was a pretence, conjured for his sake, in order to conform to a role he wished on her, and that she must live henceforth in the shadow of an intricate dishonesty?

Perhaps it was none of those things, but only the slow steady force of infidelity, which loosened one by one the sinews of life, and made, even of the greatest hero, such a ruin as Guy now was. Mary often prayed for him to the God in whom she did not believe. At times, sitting alone in the study next to her bedroom, which had been her father's study and her grandfather's before him, and hearing Guy as he stumbled about the house in search of whisky, she would be acutely conscious of his failure to belong among her family ghosts, and she would pity him. She had brought him here, like a castaway, only to rouse him to a place already too much possessed, a place in which objects had been handed down from generation to generation until they were worn smooth by ownership, and retreated from the stranger's touch. She had offered no home, but only hospitality. And the world outside had offered less.

"It's a funny thing," Guy was saying, "the way women accept mistreatment, once they know that no other treatment is available. It is very bad for us, very bad." And he shook his head slowly, so that the bald patch that crowned his skull briefly caught the light from the window and glowed like a moon. Guy was good-looking still, with an angular profile, deep set brown eyes, and an expression of suffering and resolve that bore no relation to his character, but which opened door after door for him into places of failure. It was surely his face that had led to the disastrous two months with the London Bach Ensemble, during which his incompetence as a conductor had been proved to everyone save himself. It was certainly his face that had led to his being taken up by Penelope Sterndale, so that he could roam among her modernist furnishings on Thursday evenings, amid gurus and moguls and the well-heeled avant-garde. And it was his face that caused so much trouble among Penelope's chorus of women.

"If you are stopping by at the Campo dei Fiori," Guy said, "you must give my regards to La Berganza—you know, the old lady who used to call me 'signorino' and who would peel the baby onions when I bought them for your lunch. Of course, you won't need to go there now; I expect Piero will have everything laid on."

When she had left Piero for Guy, seven years ago, Mary had taken a calculated risk. Guy was a would-be and a might-have-been, whose musical career had seen few successes; whereas Piero was the rising star of the Italian film industry, the director tipped to win the Leone prize, whose *Adagio Cantabile* had stirred so many Italian hearts with its portrait of the old Calabria. Piero was an accomplished lover, with an erotic fluency that filled her with renewable desire. And Piero lived freely within the confines of his ancestral religion, visiting her in the little flat by S Andrea della Valle with an easy conscience, and returning dutifully each evening to his wife, his mother and his child. But there lay the difference. For Piero, she was something expendable—a luxury that he could always discard. For Guy, who had called on her in Rome at Penelope's suggestion, she was essential—or so he said. His first appearance had the character of a summons, like the annunciation made to another Mary, in the most beautiful story she knew.

Often in those winter days, she would travel North to Florence, to stand before Simone Martini's painting in the Uffizi. And in the retreating form of Christ's mother, she discerned the mystery of her own existence—not what she was, but what she would have been, had fate been kind to her. Even in the tenderest embraces, she held her inner being so—curled in upon itself, compact, inviolable. She had yet to make a gift of her inner life, since she set its worth too high for easy conquest. And it was this inner life that Guy had addressed, as he stood on the threshold and directed his dark gaze towards eyes that hesitated for a moment to return his look and then yielded completely. Within minutes they were making love on the couch beside the window, the evening sunlight sparkling in his light brown hair, and the noise of the street, as the restaurant shutters opened and the cobbles squealed under home-going scooters, set them apart from humanity, as though they lived in moments, not in days.

"Take my advice though, Mary. If Piero wants to marry you, now that his mother is dead and his daughter stowed away in that convenient hospital, he will have to be fitted out with a mistress. He is a two-woman man, which makes him five times less fickle than me, but twice as fickle as the ideal husband."

When she got to Rome, she would sell the flat and travel. She had never seen Calabria, the Calabria glamorized in *Adagio Cantabile*. She wondered what had become of Piero, now that his schizophrenic daughter had been removed from him. They had learned of the tragedy from a film magazine, which reported that Piero and his wife were living apart, and that his great *Life of the Magdalene* had been left unfinished when the leading actress, with whom he was having the affair required by their successful cooperation, had—as a result of his attentions—swollen to an unacceptable size.

Perhaps the greatest of her mistakes had been the first one, of bringing Guy home with her. In Italy, he had lived in poverty as a would-be composer, while in England he had merely failed at more promising careers. But it was an established principle with the Durbridges that the head of the family should reside in the old house in Kensington, and upon her father's sudden death she found herself, age twenty-five, head of the family. Her first novel had been accepted by a London publisher, and the thought of this success was too thrilling to forego the chance of enjoying it. Five novels later she saw how damaging it had been, to deprive Guy of the subterfuges whereby he had gone on believing in his creative powers. By then it was too late, and she had ceased to enjoy her own success, so much did it emphasize his lack of it.

"I don't suppose it matters, if he doesn't make that blasphemous film. He has had his moment of glory without spitting on the altar at which his grandmother prayed. Don't think I'm jealous, by the way. I've declined beyond that point."

He laughed quietly to himself. A faint murmur of car-tyres in the street took up the sound and carried it around the corner. Silence. To her surprise, Mary was irritated at the sight of Guy's abandoned whisky glasses, which lay about the room, glinting in the semi-darkness, and leaving sticky rings on marquetry heirlooms. He was not an oaf, but he made himself oafish, since this was his way of showing that he did not belong. Now that she was leaving the house to him, none of this should matter. But it mattered very much, and she had to fight against her anger, lest it spill out in words. Guy was allowed everything save words, which were too precious to put where they might be trampled on.

"A funny thing about the Italians, this need for blasphemy. Their last attempt to hold on to their faith, by mocking it. You should try it some time. Are you still there?"

He turned suddenly in his chair and looked into the darkness of the house. His eyes had the urgent concentration of a trapped animal.

"Ah, there you are, loitering in doorways. Never deciding to enter or to leave a room, but poised always on the threshold. I won't say it doesn't suit you. You are a threshold sort of person, the sort of person who must be pushed aside by those who storm from the room."

Once, it is true, he had pushed her. They were on the Welsh border, where Mary borrowed a cottage from Rebecca Stanton, the cookery writer—a sweet, homespun place with slate tiles and whitewashed walls of stone. A stream chuckled past in the valley, and a hill rose behind, its green gauze buttoned with sheep. Mary loved the cottage, had come here every year since university, always alone until Guy appeared. She had her own desk, which Rebecca left untouched and on which piles of paper lay from year to year, ready for Mary's pen and yellowing beneath the dormer window. That summer she was working well; Guy had been commissioned to write a string quartet and was installed downstairs at Rebecca's worktable. They met for walks and meals, and conversed about simple things. And the love and praise of God arose within her, like a flower. They attended the Anglican church on the hill, sang the hymns, his strong tenor resounding above the cracked voices of the old parishioners, even knelt together in prayer. They sat side by side at night, listening to the tawny owl as it lifted the flap of darkness. She held his hand and felt in his soft palm the smile she could not see. She was wife to him in all but name, and when he came one day to find her and saw the Book of Common Prayer lying open at the marriage ceremony, he gave her a yielding look. Perhaps he would have spoken but she, in her embarrassment, pushed the book away and picked up her pen. It had always been a fault of the Durbridges that they could not make conditions, but waited and waited until the time for decisions had passed.

It had happened later on the same day. She was standing at the bottom of the staircase, looking across the oak-beamed room to the table where he worked, splinters of sunlight lying on his hands. The pages of music paper were blank, save for a few black notes in a corner. His hands were still, and his face was turned from her towards the window. A faint breeze rustled the pines outside, and their branches soothed his profile like the hands of a woman. The tenderness that invaded her was not for Guy only, but for herself as Guy's lover and for the soft growing sphere of their love. And maybe it was the hope that flowed from her that so annoyed him. For she said nothing, did nothing, as she stood observing him, was even on the point of turning back to her attic when, with a bound, he rose to his feet and sprinted towards her.

A cold-pinched anger clawed his features. The storm-trooper eyes bored through her like bayonets, and a snarl tore open his face. She shrank against the door frame. And then, with one pouncing movement, he took hold of her in both his arms and pushed her backwards on to the stairs. He slammed the door between them, and shouted "yes, yes, I'm sorry, I'm sorry!" as though to drown her tears. Later she heard him pacing around the living room, muttering to himself. But when she came down for supper he smiled at her as though nothing had happened.

"You will have to become a communist, of course. There's no advancing in Italian society without the red badge of cowardice. I would have done the same, had I stayed there. The trouble is, I'm the kind of person who merely pretends to be a phony. And because people know that I'm pretending, they take me for a phony, when I am not a phony at all, but only pretending. You, on the other hand..."

He broke off, swallowed from his glass and spluttered. The paroxysm shook his body and she noticed, as he bent backwards and forwards, how frail he was. Almost nothing remained of his shoulders save a drooping curve of bone, on which the loose grey cardigan hung like a sack. Once, she had enjoyed Guy's careless way of dressing. Then he had seemed proud, spiritual, with a direct line to other humans that bypassed outward forms. In time, however, she had begun to resent it. As his drinking increased, Guy's body deteriorated. His shabby clothes became the more dispiriting, since they revealed his ruin and also, in their own way, rejoiced in it. You are coming home to us, they seemed to say, joining us on the dust-heap of history.

He leaned back in his chair with a gasp, and then was still.

"No. Nobody could call you a phony. Your deceptions are not carried out against the world, but only against a few carefully targeted individuals, and of course only for their comfort and peace of mind. I admire that. It has a civilised feel to it. Your lies are whiter than white, soap-powder white."

At first, she had meant to tell him about Robert. It would have cleared the air, opened the path to his atonement, by way of her own atonement. For God knows Guy needed to make amends. Not only for the obvious things—the violence, the abuse, the affairs which were not the less hurtful for being often imaginary, since it was precisely through his imagination that he chose to injure her. He needed to make amends for those things that only she had seen and suffered. The refusal, in so many ways, to make marriage into a live possibility, knowing that she craved this blessing, and that her frail faith would give way without it, as it did at last on that day in Cirencester. She recalled his habit of arriving late for her dinner parties, as though he were just another guest, one with more urgent engagements who had condescended to turn up, nevertheless, in the hope of some casual liaison. Once, sitting between Rebecca Stanton and the Philpot girl—where she had placed him precisely so as to emphasize that they were a couple and must therefore sit apart—he had entertained his neighbours in a loud and barking voice with a description of his week in the recording studio. She did not know how sincere the description was, though it cast great credit on him and prepared his listeners for the judgement that, were the CD of his symphony never to appear—which of course it never did—it would not be the fault of the composer. But she was amazed that she was never mentioned in the story—she who had come with him each day, who had sat through hour upon hour of dismal repetition, who had smiled encouragement at the most cacophonous moments, all the time suppressing her desire to run from the studio and wash out her ears with Haydn or Bach.

"In a way your life has been a work of art, as neat and smooth as your novels. Useless and perfect as a diamond. My life on the other hand—well, what has it been but a spoof? A farce on the life of Beethoven, written by the team that brought you *Star Trek*. You know what was the most stupid thing I tried to do?

The most all-out fucking criminal act of self-destruction I ever embarked on? It was writing that Mass in C minor. A Mass in C minor, in 1988, the time of Thatcher and Gorbachev and TV soaps and heavy metal bands—a postmodern confession of faith, a requiem for God, including all his favourite tunes with due acknowledgement to the Devil, who wrote the best ones. I must have been stark fucking crazy!"

The Mass had only one performance. It was in St. John's, Smith Square, with the Britten singers and a little orchestra Guy had scratched together from his students. She had formed the resolution to tell him about Robert. They would slip away after the concert, to dinner at the Golden Cornet where they had celebrated their little successes—she her novels, and he the two quartets from his early days. He would know that she was offering her life to him, making her confession so as to give him the right to choose. And the Mass would cast its benign light over their loving kindness, as first she, then he, sought true forgiveness from each other.

But when, in the all but empty concert hall that had once been a church, the choir faltered through those antiquated harmonies, and Guy's sad face froze over in despair, she abruptly changed her mind. Mary was not musical. But she heard how limp and flat and easy were the notes dolled up by the choir. And she sensed the insincerity of the composer, who was papering over his lack of faith with these pious clichés. *Agnus Dei, qui tollis peccata mundi*—the lovely words, which contain within themselves the whole mystery of the Christian religion, its power both to trouble and to soothe, to imbue the soul with humility and gratitude, to capture in one rhythmic phrase the astonishing truth of our redemption—these words, in Guy's setting, were chanted like an advertising jingle over white chords on harp and vibes and glockenspiel, the vibraphone being the only concession that he made to contemporary fashions. And yes, precisely because he made so few concessions, the music had lost its sense. It spoke neither to our world nor to the world from which it borrowed its worn-out gestures. It was pale and insubstantial as a ghost, and its bloodless sounds were both ridiculous and chilling in their emptiness. Mary left the church at his side in silence. They walked through winter streets, while she sought in vain for words to console him.

"It was a confession, of course. A confession to you. The music said it all—how childish and empty and self-deluded. O.K., it was a notch better than 'Kumbaya, My Lord,' and it *was* in a minor key. But it shouldn't have been in *any* key. Keys are chains. The worst thing about it was that it brought me face to face with the truth. Who wants to be face to face with anything, let alone the truth? I realized that music can be as deceitful as any other art—as deceitful as those sentimental films of Piero's."

Yes, that was when it really happened. That was the moment when he had changed, the moment when she had become his enemy. He ceased then to share his griefs, or even to confess to them, opting instead for an insolent contempt towards her, and a flaunting of his carefully nurtured vices. One by one the blows rained down on him, and he received them all with an asinine cheerfulness that was appalling to behold. Yet in everything he depended on her; she was the source of guilt, without which he could not believe in his creative powers; and she produced food, drink, and shelter, which he snatched from her angrily, lest the thought should arise in him of his shameful sponging.

He was coughing again, bent forward in the armchair, his

left hand on his chest. Her eyes rested for a moment on the damask curtains, gathered into the casement and softly glowing in the light from outside. Her father, in his bereavement, had kept them closed for two years. The room was to keep vigil over Mummy's things, until the thought of her absence could be borne. And when he died, Mary came home from Italy, and the curtains were opened. That was the first change. The second was Guy, who had broken and abused Mummy's furniture, and filled the room with his drink and his anger and his noise. The Durbridge ghosts had fled his presence, and now she too was fleeing. Yet this usurper could not survive alone, and in leaving him she was condemning him. He gasped and half turned in her direction.

"I never got to the bottom of this religion thing. I was embarrassed and bewildered at first, when I saw you praying. After all, you were the normal sixties product; you had slept around, indulged yourself, taken no interest whatsoever in the poor in spirit and the pure in heart. You were as greedily into me as you had been into Piero, and no fasting or penitence was on the menu that I could see. But you wanted me to believe, and I got the knack of pretending, waiting for the reason why."

It was love that made her believe—love for Guy, and also the love of home and parents and childhood, and the deep down need to return to the place where wounds could be tended and fears overcome. He wrecked that place, like a rampaging soldier, and raped and strangled the loving child in her. She had turned to Robert as one hardened adult turns to another, without hope or faith or charity, but only desire. Had she told Guy of the affair when she intended, she could have relinquished it; there would have been hope of a kind, faith of a kind, and the charity they deeply needed. But it was the Mass that stood between them. Not Guy's music only, but the holy words that he abused. Only if they had gone down on their knees in mutual penitence could their love have been saved. But the Mass forbad them. It was spoken into regions from which their souls had fled.

And because she had not confessed her fault, the visits to Robert continued. She would enter his office in the city, in the forlorn and silent hour when the secretaries had left for the suburbs, and cast her body like a ransom on the woollen carpet. They exchanged few words, and she was grateful for this, for Robert thought and spoke accountancy, and she dreaded the moment when he might weigh up the cost. Robert had no understanding of art and literature, no time for religious hesitations, no ability to perceive the quiet residue of pastness that she looked for everywhere, like one gathering flowers in a building-site. But he admired Mary. His desire was a tribute to her strangeness; she was for him an icon of the spiritual life, of all the things that were impassably remote from his concerns, but which mattered in ways that he could only guess. He would rise from the floor bearing on his square-jawed face an expression of boyish tenderness, as incongruous as a poem on the lips of a bear. It wanted only a moment's thought for his desire to crystallize as love, for the vast bullying resources of his ego to lean towards absolute possession, and for the cost of her remoteness to become unbearable. Robert was successful because he was ruthless and would tolerate no expenditure that did not lead to profit. She fled from his presence before his investor's instincts could be aroused. For he could never be anything to her beyond these moments of eager pleasure in the city stratosphere, where they floated in a dream, buoyed aloft on the unreal clouds of commerce. Even the thought of meeting Robert elsewhere, of encountering him on terra firma, of knowing his earthly presence as woman knows the reality of man, was abhorrent to her. And thinking of this, she felt a wave of revulsion at her betrayal—a betrayal not of Guy only, but of herself.

"I heard you packing, by the way. Sounds as though you plan to take some of the books. Don't go to any unnecessary trouble. I'll be out of here in a fortnight, and you can return, enjoy your position as the heir to the house of Durbridge. It would do me good to live elsewhere. Shit!"

He spluttered again, this time so violently that the glass fell from his hand on to the carpet. She stepped forward, then regretted her instinct and stood still. There was a curious sound upstairs—a faint padding of slippered feet, and a mumbled monologue, as though some mad old person were patrolling one of the bedrooms. Often in recent days, she had heard this sound. She put it down to her indecision. She had read of a woman who, having made up her mind to live apart from her husband, had found herself impeded by imaginary people. They would stop her in the street, give advice on irrelevant subjects and detain her with trivia. She had encountered them at home, sitting in familiar chairs and addressing the air with songs and news stories and shopping lists. And when one morning she awoke to discover that her intentions had changed, and that it was no longer on the cards to leave her husband, the visitors vanished, their mission achieved.

The sound persisted. It was no longer a faint shuffling in a bedroom, but a definite footstep on the landing, as though the hermit of those upper regions had been moved to investigate their grief. She thought of the house and its dead and felt a chill.

Perhaps she was going mad. Perhaps nothing that she heard or saw or did was really real. If only Guy would love and protect her: it was all she asked for, although she could not bring herself to ask. Suddenly a voice whispered.

"Mary."

She turned and looked into the stairwell. A light shone from her bedroom door, and the Chinese vase which stood on the landing table glittered with red and gold flames. The footsteps had ceased. Nothing moved. Silence. She shuddered and turned back to Guy.

"Mary."

What was it that startled her? The tenderness, the need for her, the promise of love, how strange they sounded in this room, where love had died. Who was it, reaching out to her in this dark abyss? She thought of her father—a frail, grey, broken man, a magenta dressing-gown pulled tight around his crumbling body, his lips thin, sad and stoical beneath the military moustache. He had been her refuge from the storms of childhood, and his rare smiles were for her. Invalided out of the army, he had spent his days at his desk, composing appeals to people in high places, who wrote back out of respect for the name of Durbridge, but with words that could not console. Now he was back, speaking to her in the soft and all-forgiving voice that he reserved exclusively for her.

"Mary."

No. It was not her father's voice. Yet it was spoken into her heart and trembled with concern for her. Guy's voice too had trembled, for the year or two when they lived in this house as sovereigns, bowing and retreating at the untouchable majesty of love. They had looked on each other with awe. She hesitated to enter the room where he sat, so full was it of his presence. Every gesture was an offering, and they laid out their words as gifts. What had happened was not Guy's fault but hers. It was she who, on that fateful day which for some reason she only now remembered, had doubted the reality of their love. It was she who, closing her notebook for the morning, with the thousand precious words completed and stored, had come down to where he sat, and condemned his willed sterility. How queer and grey and anxious was his face, as he raised it from the desk. He had asked her what she meant, and all of a sudden and without warning, a torrent of grievances rose within her and spilled over into words. He was not a husband to her, scarcely a lover, so preoccupied was he with *his* affairs, or lack of them. He had no concern for her work, her hopes, her loneliness, even her daily survival. O.K. he knew how to cook. But when did he sit down and converse with her? When did he share the anxiety that consumed and destroyed him? Foolishly, she mentioned their religion, suggested counselling, a visit to Rory Backhouse, the Anglican monk who practised his own kind of brow-soothing therapy in the resurrected monastery of Purfield, and who had been an army friend of her father's.

"Do you think that will work?" he cried. "Do you really think that will work on *me*, a person with a brain and a smattering of scientific knowledge? Am I likely to sit with arms folded and eyes closed while some phony old Etonian puts his hands on my head and mumbles, and believe that he is purging me of my devils? Anyway, I *like* my devils. They are *mine*, made in my own image. In a certain manner, they're all I've got."

At once he took her hand and begged forgiveness, promised to mend his ways, promised even to visit Brother Rory. But she could not forgive him. From his beseeching looks that day she turned in silence.

Suddenly the room was plunged into darkness. She shrank against the wall. A few shards of light gathered in the window, and Guy's head was etched against them. The street-lamp flickered, cast a quick shaft of yellow on the carpet, and went out again.

"Mary."

The one who spoke her name had need of darkness. He was the god of terrors, not the god in whom she once believed, but a god who lived inside her like a worm. He knew her faults and conspired to double them. He led her into danger and vanished when she turned for help. There was no weapon that could vanquish him, save steadfast love: the love that she had thrown away. Silence: as though the house were holding its breath. Mary was on all fours, crawling toward him. How good he had been to her; how gentle and forgiving as he tended her wounds. Never until today had he sneered at Piero, though God knows Piero deserved it. Instead, he had lifted her carefully like some rare plant from the swamp in which she had fallen, and shaken her roots free of the slime. It was he who must forgive her—now, this instant, before the god prevented her.

"Mary."

The voice was in the room now, seeking her out, owning the darkness. She was sweating as she crawled along the carpet; the smell of dust and shoes tickled her nostrils. If she could reach him, she was safe. She wondered why he did not speak. Was he so drunk that he noticed nothing, not even the darkness? She must hold his hand.

"Mary."

She reached the chair, and fumbled along the arm in search of his hand. She knew now that it was Guy who spoke, that the pretence was over for him as it was for her. She took his hand and pulled it away from the chest. It fell heavily towards her. She was surprised by its weight.

"Guy," she said. "Forgive me. I want to stay with you. Always."

He did not move, nor did he respond to the pressure of her fingers. His hand lay in hers like a fruit dropped from the bough. The fingers were stiff crops of cartilage, which sprang back against her as she squeezed them. She replaced the hand across his body, and again she was surprised by the weight of it. As she touched the dishevelled cardigan a sadness came over her. Guy's shabbiness was after all the signal of his need. She let her hand rest for a moment on his chest and looked up at his face, grey and barely visible.

The eyes were closed, and on the craggy cheeks two tears were shining. She rose on her knees, to study his features in their sudden repose. And an image came into her mind of the view from the street of these silent figures, poised in the act of repossession, coming home to each other, weary, loving, reconciled.

From outside there is no part of human life that is not mysterious, as a closed warehouse in a suburb is mysterious after dark, even to those who work there. Most mysterious of all is love: not the love that shows itself in the disco or on the park bench, but the love that precisely does not show itself, being glimpsed through a window, or implied when a curtain is drawn. And of all these secret loves, none is more mysterious than that which is most common—the love of the family from which strangers are shut out. This is where God shows himself, at the place where human beings hide. In her imagination, she saw herself and Guy frozen into a religious icon, all their strife redeemed. And suddenly, easily, her faith returned. She could not frame it in words. But it was real—as real as the memory of their country church, where a chancel light lay in pools about them as they prayed.

"Oh Guy," she said.

But his eyes did not open. Upstairs she heard a door softly close, as though someone were returning to his room. And by the dead body of the man who would not marry her, she knelt in prayer.

Sarah

SHE WAS STANDING OUTSIDE THE CLASSROOM in which he had finished lecturing on the Holy Sonnets of Donne: a girl of no special beauty, but with a fresh, serious expression in her grey eyes, and an earnest upturned face that seemed to ask for instruction.

"Are you waiting for me?" he asked.

She nodded, and fell in step beside him, like a dog. Her feet were cased in leather hiking boots, and she wore black tights beneath a sober skirt of blue cotton. A kit-bag swung from her shoulder, and she held its strap with her right hand as she walked.

Haldane College was built in the nineteen thirties, with long corridors and glass-panelled doors of varnished pine. To reach Harold Strickland's office, it was necessary to descend two flights of steps on which a continuous crowd of students flooded to and from the classrooms. Many of them stared at Harold; some gave a distant greeting. He tried to make it appear as though the girl who followed at his heels had nothing to do with him. He neither spoke to her as they descended nor looked in her direction. But he was conscious of her eyes and of the step that she matched to his exactly.

"This is where I work," he said.

It was impossible to enter the room in any elegant or welcoming manner, since the door was kept shut by a fire-hinge, and had to be held ajar with one foot while quickly sliding the other forward. The operation was made doubly difficult by the books that Harold carried in his arms, and by the necessity to prop the door open as he passed beyond it, so that the girl too could slide through. The effect of their two bodies wriggling together into the private space beyond was like an illicit intimacy. Standing at last in the space of the office, he felt compromised before her. Yet he had often entered here with others and felt no such thing. There was something in the look that she gave him, from her wide-open unblinking eyes, that unnerved him.

"What can I do for you?" he said at last.

"Can I sit down?"

"Please do."

He brought up a chair from the wall, and placed it so that she could face him across the desk. But she retreated to the wall and sat against it in another chair. Her hair was close-cropped, and she swept her hand across it with a boyish gesture.

"I don't think you are one of my students."

"No. Though I was hoping...I..."

"It is probably too late to take the course."

"I was hoping..."

"Though if you want to sit in, I've no objection."

"I was hoping you would prove that I exist."

It was the kind of remark that students spring on their teachers. But from her lips it sounded like a confession. She looked at Harold as though she had come through to him after weeks of struggle. Her accent was childish, and the pale hands on her lap were the hands of a child.

"I am not sure I can help."

"No. Only, there's no one else."

"What makes you so sure?"

She looked at him as though amazed that he could have any doubts in the matter.

"Because everyone else is shit," she said in a whisper.

Harold looked from the window. In the thin November sunshine, the yellow brick of Haldane College seemed sulphurous, volcanic, as though thrown up by some great eruption. A seagull swooped and hovered high above the inner quadrangle, and he fixed his eyes on it. The girl was tempting him, not with her charms, but with his own self-image. And of all temptations, this was the hardest.

He thought of Judy, the graduate student whom he had recently married, and how cleverly and cautiously she had trodden around him, overturning nothing, hiding from him, allowing him to stand and breathe, like a lioness tracking her prey, until he had turned at bay and surrendered. Judy had lifted his daily burdens; she had made him appear normal, blameless, entitled to his share of space and time. Confronted by the present emergency, Harold reached out for older and less innocent habits.

He turned back to the girl, who was still watching with a wide-eyed and helpless gaze. He asked her name.

"Sarah."

"And you are a student here?"

"Sort of. I mean my boyfriend is. My other name's Oldcastle. I'm supposed to start next year. Ex-boyfriend, I mean. Things got in the way."

She paused for breath and then swallowed. Books, papers, furniture, all fled the space where she sat and her wounded face was framed before him. The pale parted lips sucked on the air and the eyes, like pools, gazed steadily upwards. Not once had she smiled; no signals had escaped her that would permit him to treat her presence as anything less than a catastrophe. "Why me?" he wanted to ask, but the question seemed selfish and trivial.

He rose from the desk to arrange his books on the shelf behind it. But the row of tired volumes offered no relief. The standard editions, standard critics, set texts and study guides, the bound volumes of *Scrutiny*, now dumb as a priest with Alzheimer's—so many ghosts that beckoned from the world of adolescence. He contemplated them with nausea. He felt her eyes on his back, eyes that called for his face as a pool in the dusk calls to the bird that circles it. The cycle of his days, from book-lined room to book-lined room and back again, the anxiety, the sense of waste, of a mission that refuses to crystallize in a coherent goal, of a mistake once made which could not be remedied since it was neither his nor anyone's, the knowledge that nothing of value could emerge from this life of scholarship, while no course of action seemed possible, save the futile stirring of an anger which he did not deserve or deserved, if at all, only for having stirred it—all this, which he knew, because he had no illusions, was nothing more than the dissatisfaction of the species with the sterile life of Harold Strickland, but which was prompting him always towards the maddest caprice so as to imagine even a last-ditch rescue of God Himself—all this surged in him and would not be denied. He turned and went across to her.

"And what makes you think that I'm not shit?"

"I know," she whispered, "Cos I read your stuff. Death, frinstance, what you wrote."

She watched him without moving. The article on death was one of his weekly columns in *The Daily Monitor*. The columns had created a stir. Some had praised his style, others his range. But none had praised his arguments, certainly none of what he had said about death as the good-natured foe of the welfare state. Who was going to endorse such a reactionary doctrine? Yet here was a girl ready to offer what he secretly sought: not agreement but discipleship. Harold was stunned by the discovery, as though looking in a mirror to confront a face not his own.

"So how am I to prove that you exist?"

"Just tell me to go away."

Of course, that is what he should do. Wisdom and ambition, the principles that he was given to defending, his marriage, all endorsed Sarah's plea. It thrilled him to defy so many imperatives, for the sake of a whim.

He was standing in front of her, his hand on the blue serge jacket that covered her shoulder. The material was coarse, firm, newly woven. She lifted her head slightly, stretching her neck as though expecting him to touch it. Her skin was smooth, unblemished, almost as white as the shirt-collar that lay against it.

"I can't prove your existence. Only you can do that."

She did not respond, but merely continued to stare up at him.

"But maybe there's something else. Something more concrete, some problem in particular."

He laughed inwardly at his own words. All problems are concrete, but it is the fate of adolescence to dress them in abstraction, so that the week's rent, the blocked drain, the failed date, the angry parent, the bad trip, the hangover, or the unfinished essay become proof of the boundless futility of existence, and the imminent ending of the world.

"There's lots of them I can't say so I've written them down, things gone wrong. Heaps of. You can read them."

Ignoring the hand on her lapel, she leaned quickly forward and opened the strings of the kit-bag. It contained books, papers, two apples and a crumpled shirt. She fished a brown envelope from the muddle and held it out to him. He took it from her and went back to the desk.

Inside were three sheets of white paper, covered in italic writing that leaned forward, then backward, as though blown about by the wind. She watched motionless as he read.

I was properly brought up; two parents, sister, older brother, dad at work, Roman Catholic, meat and two veg, grammar school, we even had Greek. This was in Norfolk, King's Lynn, miles from anywhere, and the sea each morning, with its breeze and clouds. Then mum died, just like that, stiff under the clothes-line when I came home from school, with Dad's dungarees fanning her body like a bird. I didn't cry. I didn't run for the ambulance or the priest. I just went indoors and ate the cake she had left on the table. I loved her cakes, and this was the last one. There was nothing I could do in any case, since I was to blame for her death. That was how I saw it. The next day I tried to join her, but they rescued me with stomach pumps. I'm telling you this because you'll understand. Nobody understood before—not even Emily, my little sister. She told me I was seeking attention, that I was too selfish to see there was nothing special about my grief, compared with her grief, or Dad's or Richard's. I guess she was right. Except that I was to blame. But how could I explain that?

Then I started having these revelations. Don't get me wrong. I don't believe in God—not anymore. But he kept talking to me—rousing himself from his nonexistence all heavy with sleep, and confiding in me. He had a scheme for his resurrection, and I was to play an important part. Not spreading the gospel or anything; just living a pure life, and atoning for what I'd done. Then, by a miracle, things would make sense again. I imagined him being reborn in a corner of my room, among the sneakers and gum-boots. He would be yellow and shrivelled at first, with half-closed eyes like a Chinaman. But then he would grow to fill the house.

Dad started bringing this woman home. Her name was Lisa and she smelt of roses and sweat. Mum had brought us up on Mozart and Schubert. But now he sat in the living room listening to Petula Clark and Frank Sinatra, holding hands with this moron in crinoline. God told me not to talk to them. I stayed upstairs, reading and learning Arabic. Emily brought me my meals, and this bloke from school would visit me, though I didn't let him get very far. Only he was Lebanese, and told me about his country and the situation of the Christians there. That was why I was learning

Arabic. I wanted to understand this strange thing—this bearing witness in the land of Christ. A vision came one day and it helped me. I saw a rocky hillside with scrubby trees and a few goats and on the summit a square stone church with a few stone buildings scattered around it. Everything was bathed in a yellow light, and a figure stood in the porch of the church with his arms outstretched. He wore long blue priestly robes, and blood was pouring from a wound in his chest. He was asking me to come to him. All of a sudden, life had meaning again. I had been singled out as a person whose life was worth risking. I know you will understand this. You wrote something once which really struck me. You said that life has meaning only to the one who is prepared to give it away, and for no other reason than that it has been asked for. That made sense of so many things for me. When I look at my age-group, I see that nobody could possibly ask of them the slightest sacrifice, and certainly not that one. Not because they are determined to hang on to what they have, but because they have nothing to give. Giving is foreign to them, a thing of the past, like fox-trots, tea-parties and the Book of Common Prayer. (How do I know about these things? Because of you.)

I finished school that year, and had decided on Haldane College, because you were there. Richard had already gone to Oxford, and Dad was going to be married to Lisa. Emily was waitressing and got herself pregnant by one of the cooks. I had to leave home, and the easiest way was university. But first, I must go to Lebanon. It was decided for me in big gothic letters, on a bright blue sky. Then this other bloke I'd met at a party wrote to me, and said he was going to study at Haldane and had got himself a flat. He asked me to share with him, and it seemed like a good idea. A step on the way. I did some waitressing over the summer, saved enough for a few months in London, and came to live with him. He was my boyfriend for a bit. I had no courage for anything else. I began hanging around the college and the libraries, and everything became a mess. Jim—that was his name—began to disgust me with his stupid music and his spoiled ways, lying in bed all day with those earphones on his head, sponging off his friends, not interested even in studying, and so often rude as they all were about you. I had to leave, and I felt my weakness. But there was no one to talk to, and I began to regret that I'd put off Haldane until next year.

Then a new vision came. That vision was you. Jim took tapes of your lectures and brought them home; I began to follow them. I read the texts, and they sounded in your voice in my mind. At last I knew what poetry was about. And there was such a strength and conviction in your words—it all seemed to matter so much to you. If you are reading this, then it is because I have plucked up the courage to give it to you. God knows what will happen now. Perhaps you will tell me to go away. That would be best. Only I had to see you.

Harold raised his eyes from the page and tried to smile at her. But he managed only a clenching of the brow. Sarah leaned backwards so that her head touched the wall, and her neck stretched to its full extent, like the white neck of a swan in flight. She was holding her breath, and her cheeks were pale.

"You should have come to see me before. It would have made things easier."

"Only everything went wrong and I couldn't make up my mind because of this vision thing which always got in the way and now you hate me."

She did not move or take her eyes from his as he came across to her. When he lifted the hand from her lap, it was cold and limp.

"I've done it with only ever one other person," she said, as he bent towards her, "and that was although I never really chose him—Jim."

Her pale parted lips were as cool as her hand, and she received his kiss as though drinking from a fountain and quenching her thirst. With closed eyes and limp body, she slid from the chair to the carpet, lifting her hands to his neck and pulling him down on top of her.

Each day, Sarah would be waiting for him. Each day, she would sit in his office in a posture of absolute obedience, sometimes reading, sometimes writing a letter which she would leave on his desk as she left. Their love-making was silent, but with a childlike eagerness, and afterwards she would look at him with a startled expression, as though waking from a dream.

She seemed to expect nothing, and this nothing began to be everything to him. His evenings with Judy were full of plans and schemes. He would apply for the Chair at Glasgow, where they could live near her parents and where she could resume work on her doctorate on the literary essays of John Stuart Mill. They would buy a second home in the Hebrides, where he could study through the summer and write. But no sooner did Sarah enter his office than all such plans and schemes would fade away. What should have been a disaster soon became a comfort, and during the quiet hours at his desk, with her canine presence undisturbed and undisturbing in the corner which he kept for her, he felt at ease with himself, relieved of every mask and costume that the world required. He may not have proved Sarah's existence, but she had certainly proved his.

He arranged for her to enrol as his student; he gave her

money, though not much since she had the art of living frugally. And together they read the books that most appealed to her— Kafka, Musil, Rilke and Proust. She spoke little, and always in a syntactical muddle that she would ingenuously unscramble with her clear, startled eyes. If she had anything important to say, it would come to him as a letter, written in the same serious and laconic style, and left on his desk or in his pigeon-hole.

They studied Arabic together, for one little plan remained in her head, which was to visit Lebanon, and to do something for the Christians there. Although the visions no longer came to her, Sarah regarded them as absolutely binding. And because of a peculiar and fateful train of events which he had disregarded at the time, but which now came to seem like a destiny, Harold concurred in her plan. Three weeks before meeting her, he had received, thanks to his weekly column, a letter from Nabil Abu Tariq, a Lebanese businessman in London, asking him to report on the civil war that had spread from the Palestinian camps around Beirut. The letter had referred to the lies that had been written in the Western press, representing the Christians as fascist war-lords, and the Muslims and Palestinians as innocent victims of a conspiracy funded by the Western powers. The writer appealed to Harold to visit the country, and to use his column to tell the truth. He decided that he would do as he was asked, and set aside a week in the Christmas vacation to accomplish it. When he finally called on Nabil Abu Tariq to make the arrangements, it was with Sarah in tow as his "research assistant."

They were shown by a shy Filipino maid into the long drawing room of a Mayfair flat. Through the tall Victorian windows, the November sun cast the shadows of plane trees, which were shaking themselves free of their leaves and baring themselves to the cold. Abu Tariq sat amid silk cushions on a low divan, staring down the length of a long powder-blue carpet towards the door through which they came. He wore a dark suit and bright red Turkish slippers of padded velvet. In his right hand was a large cigar, and he purposefully raised it to his fat lips as they entered, as though to register his unconcern. He peered at them through the screen of smoke from dark, puffy eyes, and his tanned cranium caught the light from the sloping sun and glistened beneath the strands of oily black hair like a pool of fire. Slowly, Pasha-like, he raised himself and came towards them. His handshake was limp and sweaty, and he stared at Sarah as if evaluating a piece of merchandise.

"You do me a great honour," he said, in a monotone.

"The honour is ours," Harold returned, with a self-consciously foreign smile.

Abu Tariq indicated the vast low armchairs that faced the divan and clapped his hands as they sat. Coffee was set before them, with a tray of sweet cakes.

"Your time, I know, is precious," their host continued, as he settled on to his throne. "I shall, therefore, come straight to the point."

He gestured to the cakes with a wide swing of the arm, as though to gather them up and sweep them into the mouths of his guests.

"What you read about my country in the Western press are lies. I am sure you know this. Hundreds of communities—Christian, Shi'ite and Druze, whose conscience has made them anathema to Islamic orthodoxy—have sheltered from genocide in our mountains, and we, the Maronites, have accepted our historical mission, which is to live with these refugees on terms.

That is not how your journalists see matters. To them, we are the overlords who exploit the poor Muslim masses while living in luxury in the fleshpots of Beirut. We have been allies of the West for centuries, an outpost of Christian civilisation in the midst of lawlessness and terror, and we depend on you for protection. But your journalists are destroying our credibility. Soon, no Western government will wish to intervene on our behalf. The Palestinians are creating havoc in both town and country; and the Syrians have now invaded, using our feeble attempts to defend ourselves as their excuse. And still, your journalists pour scorn on us, laughing at our humiliation from the comfort of the Commodore Hotel—a hotel, I should add, that is owned by Palestinians, and which offers every conceivable form of hospitality to these obliging guests, just so long as they write what they are told. That is why we are appealing to you."

Abu Tariq puffed on his cigar and looked at Harold. The orbs of his eyes sank behind their pouches like setting moons, and his nostrils flared slightly as he released the cloud of sweet-smelling smoke. Harold nodded and made his face look eager and serious, as though he believed what he heard and was determined to help. Already his heart was torn in just the way that it was torn by all the things that mattered. The cause of Christendom was all-important to him only because he knew that it was lost. And as Abu Tariq continued his speech, with words which had the liturgical quality that comes from the fact that no one who utters them can quite believe in their truth, he stood somewhere outside himself, looking down on the room in which he sat with his trusting slave, encouraging yet another person to trust in him. The sight fascinated and appalled him, and he followed the conversation as though he himself had scripted it, and was now toying with the uncorrected proofs.

"I'll do what I can," Harold was saying, and he glanced across to the chair where Sarah had thrown herself down like a rag-doll, with her soft white hands by her sides.

"You will understand, my dear Mr. Strickland, how interesting our position is to you and your readers. We are the only community of the Holy Catholic Church which is deeply familiar with Islamic society, with Islamic thought and Islamic law and with the language which expresses them. Islam does not recognize Christ the Saviour or the Virgin Mary or the Trinity, and therefore our dialogue with it remains, how shall we say, an existential dialogue—a dialogue of life but not of concepts. We continue to say no to Islam and shall always say no. We recognize the freedom of every conscience, the dignity of both men and women, and the equality of citizens before the law. None of these are recognized by Islam. But we have no desire to fight with our Muslim brothers, and are being pushed into this confrontation by powers which have everything to gain from extinguishing the Christian religion in our country. That is why we need your help."

Looking down from his extra-terrestrial regions, Harold foresaw nothing but disaster from this meeting; just as he had foreseen nothing but disaster from his meeting with Sarah. But he goaded his terrestrial self into a simulacrum of acceptance and promised to write the truth in the *Daily Monitor*.

"But first you must visit my country. My friends are waiting. You will have everything you need."

"I am grateful."

"It is for us to be grateful. I should add that your visit will be entirely unofficial. It is safer that way."

"Unofficial?"

"There will be no record of your entry or exit, no papers, nothing that might arouse the slightest interest among our enemies. I trust you agree to this."

Abu Tariq delivered the words in his accustomed monotone, which seemed to leave little room for dissent. Harold saw himself accept the terms with a burst of relief, for it would be easier to deprive Judy of information if his mission were clandestine. Yet this too, he knew instinctively, was inviting disaster.

"You will fly by helicopter from Larnaca. Our friends will show you what you need to see."

And so it was arranged. The day before their departure, Sarah left a letter for him.

Nobody but you could have arranged this. It will change my life and I shall never regret it. You are the only person who really exists for me. When we reach that church on the yellow hilltop, I shall know everything. I don't believe in God or angels, but an angel is with me when we are together. I shall never be a trouble to you, and when we get back, you can tell me to go away.

They found the church on the hill, and it was just as Sarah had dreamed. The priest who stood in the stone porch, his breast pierced by a bullet, cried out as they approached—though whether with a curse or a blessing they could not tell, since his words were lost in the blood-swollen sobs that were the last sounds he uttered. The man who had shot the priest was their guide, to whom they had been handed by the soldiers of the Christian militia in Souq-el-gharb. Harold's fear, which had never abated since the helicopter landed under a hail of machine gun fire in a ruined garden near Beirut, had formed a tight and immovable knot at the sight of Guillaume, as the guide styled himself. Thin, gaunt, bearded, with crazed, sunken eyes and a constant film of sweat on his upper lip, Guillaume was a young man in his mid-twenties, but with an old man's fixed expression and unyielding manner. He refused to look at Sarah, or to shake hands with Harold, but simply nodded in their direction as he negotiated with the militia soldiers who had brought them by jeep from the city. With neither a smile nor a farewell to anyone, he ordered Harold and Sarah, with a wave of the hand, to follow him. They found themselves in the cabin of an army lorry, which bumped along the pot-marked highway into the shouf. After thirty minutes of silence, Guillaume turned to Harold and informed him in idiomatic English that he was now a guest of Islamic Jihad. Sarah gripped his arm. Outside, in the April twilight, the silvery grasslands of the shouf sped past the window. The scattered villages of stone, with their square flat Maronite churches and white-washed concrete villas had been abandoned, and many of the buildings lay in heaps by the roadside.

"I don't understand," said Harold, who understood only too well. "We were guests of the Tamzin Christian militia."

"You think so?" Guillaume answered.

"I know so. They brought us from Cyprus."

Guillaume swerved to avoid an old woman who was picking her way along the road in the twilight, leading a donkey piled high with wood.

"Everyone in this country has his price, Mr Strickland. Everyone except Islamic Jihad. We are the incorruptibles. You will learn much during your time with us."

"You make it sound as though I shall be with you for quite a while."

"As long as you are useful to us."

"And my friend here?"

"She is useful too. It will make an interesting story in your newspapers."

Harold thought of Judy and the inevitable impact of this front-page news. He glanced at Sarah's pale face, and was overcome with astonishment, that he should have so artlessly brought this ruin on them all. That night, as they tried to sleep in a ruined cellar, at the door of which a guard with a machine gun murmured soporific verses from the Koran, Sarah broke her silence.

"It doesn't matter what they do to me and my family, I mean, they don't know anything or care about me anyway. So when you can, you go, that's best, and I'll delay them. I know it can be done."

He reached out and she grasped his hand. This faint, uncertain character, he knew, lived for its sudden excesses. He did not doubt that she intended another one, though how could it be done? He knew, as he lay on the bed of straw, shifting beneath the coarse military blanket that Guillaume had thrown to him, that Sarah was dispensable—that she had been sent to him precisely so that he could cast her off. And without Judy he might as well become another hostage in this land of hostages, swallowed by the animosity that grows in the no-man's land between religions. His one thought was to return to Judy and erase this winter of mistakes.

When Guillaume drove off the Damascus road and stopped

beneath the slight hill on which the village of Kafr el 'Ain had been scattered as though dropped from the sky, Sarah turned to Harold with an elated expression.

"This is the place in my dream," she said.

They were ordered down from the cabin and marched towards the church. A shot was fired behind them, and Harold fell to the ground. But it was not repeated, and when he raised his eyes, it was to see Sarah walking calmly towards the priest, who was panting out his life in the porch, his blue Melkite robes encumbering his limbs as he struggled.

Guillaume called on her to stop and began to run after her. She quickened her step, and another shot rang out as she reached the porch and plunged out of sight inside. Guillaume continued to run, beckoning to Harold and cursing in Arabic. As he disappeared into the church, Harold turned and walked, slowly at first, but then with a quickening step, towards the lorry. The keys were still on the dashboard. He had turned the vehicle round before another shot rang out, smashing the passenger window.

The road to Souq-el-Gharb was sign-posted in French and Arabic. At a crossroads, someone in military uniform waved him down; Harold made a gesture indicating urgency, and the soldier dropped his weapon. Within half an hour he had entered Souq-el-Gharb, where he abandoned the lorry and began the long steep descent to the suburbs on foot. A car slowed down and moved beside him: two young men with guns eyed him curiously from the back of it. He walked on, ignoring them. The car sped away, and was replaced by a military jeep sporting the Palestinian flag. Its open back contained a riot of young people in student dress, holding automatic weapons which they fired into the air as they passed.

At last he reached a group of drab concrete shops, in front of which people seemed to be queuing for a bus. He collapsed on to the muddy ground beside them and waited, his feelings numb with anguish and shame.

In his account to the British Ambassador that afternoon, he made no mention of Sarah and was reproached only for his peccadillo in entering such a country without a visa and in trusting to the friends of the notorious Nabil Abu Tariq.

Inside the parcel was a porcelain panel in a gold frame; painted upon it, in a Disneyish kitsch, were St. George and St. Elias, the patron saints of Lebanon. Harold sat down abruptly, pale and troubled. He did not know who had sent it, for it had been posted in Germany, and bore no return address.

"I must do something," he said. "I must go back."

"But why does it trouble you so?"

Harold looked at Judy with a desolate expression. His hands clenched and unclenched in his lap as he told the story. He described a Melkite church on a hill above the shouf, where an attempt had been made to kidnap him. To this place he had come through deserted villages, where murdered Christians lay in collective graves beside the sacked remains of their churches. It was the last outpost of our world, the shabby corner from which the web of Europe, he said, will one day be unravelled, but where the threads are still patiently rejoined each day. The path through the village was pitted by mortar shells, and the blasted vaults of Ottoman houses lay open to the spring rain, which gathered in pools where families groaned and died. Here and there in the ruined village, a candle burned beneath an icon like the one she held. A walled garden kept by nuns served the few survivors. Gourds hung on mangled carob trees, and goats, chickens, ducks, and rabbits were crammed into a tiny enclave, protected by shrapnel-torn sandbags from which the red sand dribbled like blood. He spoke briskly of the murdered priest in the porch of the church, and of his flight down the hillside, as the "Islamo-progressivist" militia made its presence known from the windows of the crumbling convent.

"Maybe those nuns are no longer alive. But they have been witnesses, seamstresses of the moral fabric. In some obscure way, we depend on them. Take them away, and there will be nothing left of our civilisation save a ghoulish pretence."

His story was odd, full of lacunae, but she accepted it as an explanation of his anguish, and begged him to take her with him, when next he should go. The flow of her love soothed and softened him; the pinched expression released its grip, and his face lay slowly calmer beneath her caresses. He let his head fall into her lap, and her hands were wet with tears. Without me, she thought, he is lost. And the thought made her happy.

Their journey was slow, confused, and uncomfortable; only five minutes before it sailed for Junieh were they granted a cabin on the ferry that plied from Larnaca. And the militia jeep which took them from the docks to the suburban bunker had room only for one beside the driver, so that Judy had to sit on Harold's lap, her neck bent at 90 degrees to her neck beneath the metal roof, as the driver gunned the machine down ruined alleys, and swerved around the craters and pot-holes that littered the streets. She collapsed on the bunk when they arrived, but was ashamed of her exhaustion. The coarse blankets smelled of urine, and the one blocked lavatory disgusted her so that she was ashamed too of her disgust. To prove herself, she insisted on going with Harold to the Green Line, where ignorant armies faced each other with grievances too old and dark to be stated in words.

On their second day, the jeep was larger, so that they could sit side by side. They were nosing down a pitted street, between old stone houses with delicate ogee arches, standing in sandbags like bath-robed beauties in their padded slippers. Behind the street, an office block had collapsed in a pile of concrete trays, from which the twisted iron fingers reached aloft imploringly. They were approaching the Green Line; the bustle of Beirut had subsided, and the streets were empty except for the few people, too old or poor to move out of danger, who scraped a ratty life among the ruins. A mile away, in Ashrafiyeh, a plume of black smoke billowed upwards into the clear blue sky, flattening out suddenly and speeding horizontally towards the shore. Judy prayed that the shell had fallen far from the car-park that they had visited, in whose concrete layers families had been crowded into cots, each with a candle-lit Madonna, and the icons of St. George and St. Elias, to safeguard what was left of home. As the shells landed in the streets nearby, the walls of the car-park flexed closer together and then recoiled again, as though a giant were cautiously prodding the sandbagged exterior with his toe. The women greeted the visitors with cardamom coffee cooked on a primus stove and pushed their groomed children into presentable lines. In their slow-moving Levantine eyes she saw Harold's face reflected, and the hope which sparked in their weary faces mirrored the hope and trust in her soul. The exhilaration of his presence was more reward than she had ever expected. She felt herself completely joined to Harold, and in the midst of the danger and the suffering, a song of love and triumph hummed in her veins. Her pity for these helpless refugees became the supreme vindication of her marriage.

He sat beside her in the jeep, his face gauzed with purpose as they approached the barricaded alleys of the Green Line: shipping containers, burned-out buses, rolling stock from the defunct coastal railway, built in Ottoman times—all had been heaped in crazy jagged piles, on which the rifle bullets slapped and ricocheted. As they entered the demarcation zone, the jeep spurted forward at full speed, the shots cracking in the air above them. A mortar-bomb exploded behind them as they darted across an exposed corner, and a few shards of shrapnel clattered on to the roof. Their destination was a narrow side-street, from which an alley wound between crumbling houses of stone and stucco into a little garden of shattered jasmine trees.

A broken door beneath a vine-clad roof yielded to Harold's shoulder, and they fell from the blazing sunlight into darkness. She made out the forms of old people lying on mattresses and wrapped in dirty sheets, their clay-like limbs protruding shapelessly from the mounds of off-white linen. The young militiaman who had shown them to the door stood guarding it in the shadow-streaked sunlight, his eyes registering no emotion as he scanned the nearby ruins, cradling his automatic across his tiny stomach. His hairless olive face, which had never known childhood, caught the rays of the sun and glowed like a lamp.

Even these people, so ruined that they are forced to live in the cross-fire, endeavour to rise at the approach of visitors, to make signs of welcome, and to beckon for the coffee that will prove them worthy of their guests—although they are beckoning only to ghosts. A smell of sweat, urine, and rotting fruit clouded the air like stale incense, and the constant murmured greeting—*ahlan wa sahlan, ahlan wa sahlan*—formed a dirge in the background. Judy looked at Harold. He was offering comfort to an old woman who held his hand and who twisted her toothless gums in a smile. It was typical of him that he had troubled to learn of this desolate refuge in the heart of war, that he had wanted to come, and that he was now beginning to record the old woman's needs in his battered pocketbook. A burst of machine gun fire ripped through the trees outside with a tearing sound, and somewhere higher up the hillside, a bomb went off with a desolate thud like a fallen statue.

A woman was moving in the shadows. She seemed young, awkward, and uncertain of herself. As she came forwards, limping slightly into the half-light, Judy noticed that her right arm hung paralyzed at her side, like the arm of a rag doll. She wore a long smock of grey serge, tucked up at the waist into a belt of string. Her face was pale, her eyes grey, wide and staring, and there was something in her posture that suggested a religious novice or a student nurse—something submissive, pious, and expectant. Harold looked up from his notebook and caught sight of the girl. The gauze of purpose was ripped from his face, and a look of terror burst like a bomb across it.

"Sarah!"

The girl stopped.

"You," she said softly, as though answering a question. Then she turned and let her eyes rest on Judy. It was a look neither of curiosity nor of assessment. It addressed Judy as a fact, a fact of the same order of magnitude as Harold, as Beirut, as the war. In those clear English eyes, Judy saw neither emotion nor judgement, but a simple recognition of herself, as the woman with Harold. But she saw something else—an abyss of misfortune and suffering into which she herself was falling.

She turned with a questioning look to Harold, who was standing rooted to the spot and silent. He took a step in the girl's direction.

"I thought you were dead."

His voice was dry, flat, beaten down by emotion.

"No such luck," the girl replied. She was holding on to a chair with her left hand, and her body swayed slightly, as though she found difficulty in standing. "I wanted to, while it was going on and the pain was worse every second, die I mean, and then I could because of you."

The short speech seemed to exhaust the girl, who panted for breath and leaned more heavily on the chair.

"But you escaped," said Harold. And this too, Judy saw, was a great misfortune.

"There were heaps of them, adventures, only I didn't think I would. See you again, I mean."

"Harold, what is this?"

Judy's cry awoke him from his trance.

"I—I'll tell you later. We must get you back to England," he went on, addressing the girl. She answered with a whispered breeze of laughter.

"You mean you want to stay?"

"This is the only place," she replied after a pause. "And there is no more in me except this thing here that's good. Who's she?"

The girl nodded at Judy with a gesture that in any other person would have been rude and dismissive, but which had the same harmless matter-of-fact quality as her every look and word.

"She—well, she's my wife."

"Oh, then you're married. Were you always married?"

Harold suddenly covered his face with his hands.

"Sarah," he groaned. He turned and began walking to the door.

"Was he always married?" The girl addressed the question now to Judy.

"We've been married for two years. Why do you ask?"

"Nobody except him deserves it, though, to be happy," the girl said, as though to herself. She subsided into the chair, and with a careful gesture lifted her right hand with her left, and let it fall into her lap. And then she sat still, looking nowhere in particular, as though waiting for whatever they had planned for her. Harold turned at the door and addressed the room with an imploring look. "*Ahlan wa sahlan,*" came mechanically from one of the beds; an old man tried in vain to raise himself on his elbow and then collapsed with a sigh; the girl did not move.

"I think we should leave," Harold said at last. "Only Sarah: why are you here?"

The girl looked up. Large, globular tears—as ingenuous and graceless as everything else about her—detached themselves from her eyelids and made their way across her face.

"It's where you would have wanted," she said and added, after a pause, "you had better go. You have a whole nother life. I can look after them."

"Forgive me Sarah," he whispered.

"There's nothing to forgive and no one's to blame because I did everything on my own."

Harold turned quickly and went through the door. The young militiaman watched him with impassive features and then got up to follow. For a moment everything was still, the rifle-shattered silence briefly healed. Judy stood in the darkened room, among those collapsed old people, her eyes fixed on the broken doll in the chair before her, her hope and her love cascading into the bottomless hollow that had opened within her. And she began to laugh, soundlessly at first, but soon with a shaking, sobbing, convulsive howl that seemed to mock the suffering around her and condemn her as an alien thing.

"Sorry," said the girl. "That sounds stupid because no one's to blame. I'm OK here. You should go."

Judy looked at her, full of hatred, not for the girl, whose undistinguished innocence made hatred as impossible as love, but for herself, for Harold, and for the poisonous fantasy which they had concocted between them and honoured with the name of love. Her laughter had subsided to a rattle of anger, but words seemed ridiculous in the face of the intolerable fact. She turned to go, shaking, aiming beyond the door, beyond the war-torn madness of the streets outside, beyond Lebanon and Harold, beyond all that she had planned and hoped and needed, to a life alone.

At the door, she paused. Something, she knew, should be said, something that would detach this scene from herself and cast it into the abyss. She forced the words between her teeth.

"Don't waste your life for his sake."

The remark was presumptuous: she knew nothing of Sarah's story, other than the catastrophe of loving Harold. But there seemed no other way to hurt the girl, who had taken all her hope away. In a second she must face him; in a second all the sordid, lying excuses would be handed to her, a plate of shit on a silver tray. She held back beneath the lintel, with the hot sun muzzling her shoulder.

"Tell him that I will write and you can read it too what happened when I can manage it. With my other arm I mean."

And Judy, who had no tears, envied the ungainly globes that sloped across those cheeks to nowhere.

Outside she began to run, Harold shouting to her from the jeep, the militiaman running after her and seizing the canvas sleeve of her jacket.

"*La!La! Khatir huna!*"

"He's telling you it's dangerous. Get in!"

She found herself beside him in the front seat as they sped along the Green Line. She pressed against the window and stared at the fleeing barricades. Above them, the bullets spent themselves in impotent slaps and howls. She could not look at him, could not speak to him, and would have stopped her ears against his vile confessions had her hands not been pressed against the dashboard.

"I understand what you feel," he said. "But it is over now, and Sarah meant nothing."

"That makes it worse," was all she said.

"What was it that I loved in Judy? O.K. "Loved" is the wrong word. What I felt for her was more than love, and also less than love. Everything about her was graceful, orderly, inherited. She had breeding, discretion, an ability to live outside the moment. She was like a promontory extended from the past over the sea of changes. I wanted to anchor myself to her, to come home to her, to be at peace with her. Even her occasional waywardness had authority for me: it was an ancestral quality, the virtue of her family of eccentrics. What in anyone else would be a sign of flux and instability, in her, was the mark of firmness. She lived above the world's opinion, needing no one's endorsement but her own. And how English she was—is, I should say, since I cannot think of her even now, except as an English lady, upright and dignified among Chippendale chairs and marquetry cabinets, and then busying herself about her studies, and on the verge of both a Ph.D. and a published monograph until the moment it ended between us. She justified me by believing in my projects. Call them quixotic if you like—I would be the first to admit the charge. But how are we, how am I, supposed to live, when everything around us is decaying? Should we do nothing? Invest our hopes in some illusion, and pursue utopias that endanger everything we have? Judy understood the point of me—she understood that a hopeless endeavour ceases to be hopeless when pursued with faith and charity. The old Pauline virtues grow together, and hope comes in the midst of despair, in the very fact of despair.

"But I failed her. She wanted all of me, even the part that was unsafe to give. I did not need Sarah. I was not even flattered by this blind devotion. But her youth spoke to my youth; she was the mirror in which I could visit my transgressions. She was time off from responsibility. Yes, and let's be frank about this, she was sex—clean, youthful, eager sex, but sex that was out of bounds, locked away and stolen. Through Sarah, I could be one step ahead of my sneering contemporaries, one step further down the path of the forbidden. I laughed at them in my soul, for their fond belief in my stuffiness and prudishness, as they pursued their sordid affairs in public. I had the greatest proof of my own liberation, in a love that could not be confessed to, not even to them.

"And then I succumbed to a greater temptation. There is a deep truth in that saying of Oscar Wilde's. I can resist anything except temptation—anything at all, for only the highest failings have ever truly appealed to me. And the appeal is irresistible. I wanted to drag this innocent love beside me into danger, to set it down in all its modern outrageousness in the middle of a religious war, among communities for whom the modern world means nothing apart from guns and bombs and horrors. To tell you the truth, I was glad when she disappeared into the church in Kafr el 'Ain, glad when that evil zombie went in search of her, glad at the thought of her lonely death in a land of which she knew nothing. She freed me from my youthful corruption, freed me from the need to prove myself through evil, freed me at last for Judy. Of course, I felt terrible too. I knew what I had done, and knew that it would scar me forever. But the scar belonged henceforth to the past. It was a wound that would heal and never again be opened. I would never have to behave in that way again.

"But my cover was blown. She did not die. They took her away for inspection: this curious and reckless creature, who had no words for them and could express herself only in writing. They tortured the arm which wrote until it could write no more. They assumed that this frail body harboured the will of a woman, and that rape, torture, and solitude would break that will. They assumed that like a good Muslim, she would crawl away from them to die. But she did not die.

"It was not Sarah who avenged herself on me, since vengeance is foreign to her nature. It was God who punished me through her destruction. Even losing Judy was less of a catastrophe than the sight of that ruined body. And then, three years later, a letter came from her. It had been posted in Turkey. I have it here.

"*You probably didn't expect me to write.*

"She always addressed me as 'you'. Never once did she indicate that I had descended so far in the scheme of things as to possess a name.

"*You probably didn't expect me to write. But I can manage with my left arm now—no good for Arabic but that's as may be. If I were a believer I would pray for your happiness with that lady. Of course there was trouble between you: how could there not be? I am sorry if I caused it. But she looked real, sensible, the kind of person who forgives. And anyway, what was there to forgive? They tried to make me hate you. As they did those terrible things to me they tried to make me believe that you were the cause of them. But I was the cause, and I want you to accept this because it is the truth. Everything changed for me when I was taken from that church. You cannot imagine what it is like, to see human beings as they are, when everything human has been removed from them and only the animal remains. No, you can imagine it, because you imagine things so well. After that, it was not possible to go back to life. I was glad that no one knew of my coming here. I have disappeared. When I look in the mirror I see nothing. There is no one there, only an absence. I have accomplished my destiny, which was to become real in loving you, and then to vanish.*

"*I am writing because I don't want you to feel bad about me. Everything happened as it should, and now that I exist only in the eye of the beholder my troubles are over. A mortar-bomb exploded in our yard, in the place where you came with her, and we had to leave, taking the survivors with us. We have a little community now, among Carmelites, North of Beirut, and we look after the old and the wounded. They have got used to the silent* inklizia *with the useless arm, and find the other arm quite helpful. Always I shall do what I can to bring peace to these people, since it is what you wanted. I have been reading the Sufis, who have weird notions. This letter will come to you through Turkey, since one of us goes that way. Should I give you my address? No, I think not; and in any case the post is dangerous.*

   "I think only of you. Be well."

"Why was I not comforted by such a letter? Precisely because she did not blame me. Because she found nothing to forgive. I lit in her a flame, and then snuffed it out. And that, for her, was all.

"It was a bad time for me. Nobody but Judy knew what had happened, and Judy had left without a word. The college made enquiries; Sarah's father replied half-heartedly, but seemed scarcely to mind that his daughter had disappeared. I kept quiet, every day expecting the scandal to break, knowing the eagerness with which it would be greeted, and retreating from my old haunts and old friendships, so as to minimize the hurt. And then a letter came from the Principal, saying that a grave complaint had been made against me, and that I must answer to charges of professional misconduct. I was summoned to his office, and went with a sinking heart. People imagined me to be hard, angry, invulnerable. Now they were going to see how easy it was to make me suffer.

"But the Principal knew nothing of Sarah. The letter he showed me had been signed by several colleagues in the English department, and related to an article in the *Monitor* in which I had argued that my colleagues had renounced academic excellence in favour of political conformity as the criterion for professional advancement. The letter might have been designed precisely to confirm my diagnosis, since it asked for my dismissal for political rather than academic reasons. Of course, my crime was described as 'professional misconduct'—but that did not disguise its true nature, as the crime of political dissent."

Harold talked on more happily, now that the matter of Sarah was clear. Recounting all this, he felt a growing tumult of relief. Sarah and Judy were both pushed aside, and in their place came a warming flood of indignation. The broken trophies of his isolation were carried upon this flood and scattered along the avenues of consciousness. Every little humiliation and indignity that he had suffered was thrown up in the volcanic storm, and delivered as a proof of good intentions. When he had finished he was laughing—not with amusement, but with anticipated triumph. Only when the paroxysm turned into a fit of coughing, which in turn necessitated a trip to the kitchen, a glass of water, and a nip of whisky from the bottle that was hidden there, did he return in his thoughts to Sarah. And he saw at once that his sufferings were no more than a farce, his isolation no better than a flight from judgement. His head ached; he was tired, exasperated, fretted to a shade by guilt that could not be shriven. He sat down heavily and raised his eyes to his friend's.

"Have you heard from Judy at all?" he asked.

The friend shook his head.

"Nobody has," he said.

Bill

MY FATHER WAS LOCAL MANAGER of an insurance firm, my mother a part-time secretary. I was an only child, and the three of us led a quiet middle-class life in a Tudorbethan villa south of Croydon. The houses in our street contained no books, other than those issued by the *Reader's Digest*. Nobody played the piano, although most households had inherited a piano from the days before the gramophone. The walls were embellished with woodland scenes in plain frames of fumed oak; and the furnishings consisted of mock-Jacobean leftovers interspersed with the latest Swedish suites in pine, chrome steel and leatherette. In short, it was a street cut off from culture, in which blameless people led more or less guilt-free lives.

In those days, when Edward Heath and Harold Wilson took it in turns to manage our political decline, our dormitory town was bounded by farms, and most of those who worked commuted to the southern suburbs of London. Our neighbours shared our routine: office, television, and Sunday outings in the car. There was a golf club, a Women's Institute, a never-ending chess tournament, and a philately circle. Occasionally someone would steal another's spouse. But such adventures, designed to render their protagonists interesting, were usually over in a month or two, when the new partner was found to be as boring as the old. There was an Anglican church, but few people attended it. Only the Catholic minority, whose church was five miles away, had much time for God, since only they believed that God had time for them. The rest of us, brought up in a vague idea that God had once checked up on the English and found them satisfactory, assumed that the relationship was best carried on at a distance. God remembered Christmas and funerals, but otherwise, like the rest of us, he kept his head down.

I attended the local grammar school and was a diligent student of the sciences, my parents having hit on science as the avenue to success in an age of technology. I had no firm view in this or any other matter, and was content to go along with their opinion. Thanks to differential calculus, I got through puberty with neither dishonour nor distinction. My days in school were spent in a cocoon of solitude, among boys from the rougher parts of town whose interests—girls and football—were impassably remote from mine.

Of course, there were other teenagers in our suburb. But

breeding was not high on the local agenda, and the few children were modelled on their parents. The boys were designed for the city, the girls for marriage. And the fact that both designs had been made obsolete by the Sixties would be discovered only later, when the children had left the assembly line and disappeared into the metropolitan chaos. When they returned, it was in pieces. The process had already begun in my sixth-form days, and one of our local wrecks, who was awaiting re-assembly in a Tudorbethan house ten down from ours, is the subject of this tale.

Bill Harrup was twenty-four when I met him in 1975— eight years my senior. He had been sent to Cambridge to study law, and afterwards to a London solicitors' office, where an army colleague of his father's was senior partner. At Cambridge, he had discovered books—poetry, history, criticism—and had attended lectures on every subject save law. He neither cared for legal work nor understood it, and would arrive so late at his desk and leave so early that his employers had been forced to sack him. An allowance from home kept him in whisky and cigarettes while he pretended to look for another job. By day, he wrote the epic poem that was to be his vindication—a modern Odyssey whose hero works his way from the alien regions of suburbia to his spiritual home in a Soho brothel. By night, he drank among drop-outs and navvies in the pubs of Kensal Green.

Bill was on his second nervous breakdown when I met him. He had been brought home by his father, having been arrested in a bookshop where he was abusing customers and removing his clothes. He was a tall, gaunt figure, very thin, and already half bald. I passed his house each day on the way to school, and would see him standing motionless in the living-room window, his hands clasped before him, and his dark hooded eyes fixed on the house across the street. His thin lips were set in an expression of resigned hostility, and his pale translucent skin clung to the bones of his face like a butcher's wrapping. The gossip was that only a last frail spasm of parental guilt stood between Bill and the loony bin, and we were all curious as to when the decision to trash him would be made.

One spring morning, to my surprise, I found him standing on the pavement as I passed his house, shifting slowly from one foot to the other, and wrapping his large parchment hands in his sleeves. Only as I passed him, and heard his body creak into motion, did I realize that he had been waiting for me. I felt no fear. On the contrary, I was overcome by a kind of troubled sympathy for the figure who strode in silence behind me. I wanted to hear his story, to endorse the experience that had brought him to this pass, and to enter into his world as a companion. But lacking words, and knowing nothing of life save its dim reflection on the TV screen, I remained silent, and welcomed him only by slowing down my pace so that he could come up beside me. However, he remained behind, as though not wanting me to see him, and when he spoke it was with an abstract, impersonal tone of voice, addressing the world in general.

"I am sitting in my ego," he said, "like a saint in a shrine."

And he laughed, a long-drawn-out and gentle laugh, an inward-turning laugh, the saddest and most solitary laugh that I had ever heard. I nodded my encouragement.

"The more perfect soul is suspended above the more fearful abyss," he went on. His tone changed to one of accusation, as immediate and personal as his previous manner had been abstract and remote. "Who wrote that?" he shouted.

"I don't know."

The words sounded stupid and defensive, and a schoolboy blush came stampeding upwards across my face.

"Maritain," he said, once more matter of fact. "And what is worse, the abyss is visible only to the one who hangs there."

His words amazed me. They suggested thought and experience far beyond our suburban boundaries. I wanted to know how you came across such words, how they could be recuperated from the debris of human speech and fitted into phrases. Who was this Maritain? Embarrassed by my ignorance, I walked on without speaking, hoping meanwhile that he would not go away. After a long pause, during which he breathed with a kind of theatrical strenuousness, Bill Harrup spoke again.

"I've seen you passing every day," he said. "Your name is Michael. Michael Sillitoe. You go to the grammar school. You are studying sciences. They will send you to Cambridge."

He spoke as though I were receiving this information for the first time. I muttered something and he came up beside me, suddenly animated.

"But you never decided on this. Your parents made the choices, and you went along with them. Isn't that right?"

Startled, I made no reply.

"Your house contains no books to speak of, save a few pulp novels. No music, save drivel from the telly set. No pictures, save a few woodland scenes and kitschy girls in cottages. Right?"

I wanted to issue a protest on my parents' behalf. But then I realised they would not regard Bill's words as criticism. So I remained without speaking.

"All the windows bricked up. Not a light-beam entering anywhere," he said, and walked on in silence. We turned a corner towards the bus-stop, and he abruptly came to a halt.

"I don't go beyond here," he said, as though declaring a policy. "But I'll tell you what. You come round this evening. Mum and Dad are playing whist. There's some whisky. O.K.?"

Then, for the first time, he looked at me, a long, unshifting gaze that seemed utterly devoid of curiosity, like the gaze of a fish.

I was not used to invitations and wondered how to reply. Before I could do so, however, he had suddenly thrust out his hand in my direction.

"Bill Harrup," he barked, as though he had just chosen a name.

I held my hand towards him, and he squeezed it painfully, before turning brusquely and walking at a rapid pace back home.

That evening we sat in his parents' living room and drank the whisky that they kept for visitors. The unfamiliar liquid descended like a flame-thrower, and I coughed in protest and pain. The Harrup living room was like ours: a chintz-covered three-piece suite; glass-topped coffee-table; glazed fireplace with pine-cones and china dogs; mass-produced prints—Vermeer, Toulouse-Lautrec, and Constable in frames of pickled oak. The bambi-bothered mantelpiece carried photographs of mum and dad, but none of Bill, whose existence was obviously negotiable. But there Bill was, resting heavy hands on spindly thighs, a figure so out of place among these visual clichés that they took on a new meaning, like words spoken on the stage.

Except when he looked up, which was rarely, his craggy brow hid his dark brown eyes. But the wrinkles around the bridge of his nose were in constant motion like waves on a rock, signalling his rapid changes of mood. At one moment he would be sunk in gloom, and at the next agitated, pouring out strings of words that continued to surprise me—words I had never heard before, or never in these strange formations.

"Let's get this straight," he said as I arrived. "I have stood my whole life long before a sea of possibilities, paddling in the shallows. And then I tripped and drowned. Some bastard gave me the kiss of life."

It was meant to be encouraging—so I decided. He seemed very old, like someone in retirement. He did not ask me about myself. Instead, he told me.

"You have hardly read anything suitable," he said. "Shakespeare, Chaucer in some ghastly modern version, maybe D.H. Lawrence and *Moby Dick*. That's as it must be, in a place like this. I suffer from drapetomania—and look at the result."

"Drapetomania?"

"A useful word," he said. "It refers to the disease discovered in slaves in the cotton fields, and consists of a pathological desire to flee from captivity."

"I haven't succumbed to it yet."

"You will, you will."

He ushered me to a chair. As he poured the whisky I noticed that his glass, which stood on the floor beside the sofa, was already almost empty. He picked up a long-playing record from the floor, placed it on a turntable behind the TV set, and dropped the needle. I was used to background music, and to parties where Buddy Holly, Adam Faith and the Beatles made conversation impossible. But Bill treated words and music in the same way—they were things to be weighed and valued. As he settled back on the sofa, he commanded silence with a wave of the hand. A most wonderful melody soared from hidden speakers. I listened in astonishment as a flute made filigree patterns around a frame of string-sound. There was a pause, and

Bill got up quickly to lift the needle.

"What was it?" I asked.

He threw the record sleeve across to me. *Orfeo ed Eurydice,* by Christoph Willibald Gluck. The name was vaguely familiar.

"The dance of the blessed spirits," he said. He pulled a string of laughter from his throat, made a flourish with his hands, and looked at me. "Blessed spirits" he repeated.

"You don't know much about music," he went on, "so you won't understand Gluck's achievement in that piece. It is not easy to express the idea of heaven: you have to transcend the world, but simply, quietly, without the least hesitation."

"Are you religious?" I asked, uncertain whether the question were permissible.

"Religious! I like that."

He laughed again, a laugh without humour, which seemed to be directed against himself. And as he laughed, he rocked back and forth on the sofa, his big dry hands beating the air as though to fend off marauding birds. Through his gestures, he seemed to mock his own existence. But his words were deadly serious, with urgent messages that I must receive while there was time.

"It is true that I have always relished solitude. But then I asked myself one day—against whom is this solitude directed?"

I could find no response to Bill's sentences. But one thing was clear to me—Bill was not mad at all. I was convinced that he had seen something, felt something, that the world denied. He had broken through the paper walls of our suburb and peered into infinite space. I was amazed and flattered that he should have chosen me to receive his confessions. All at once, my vision of myself was transformed. I ceased to be a schoolboy swot and became an outsider, standing with Bill against my parents' world.

"You must acquire precise ideas," Bill said, "but only about things that matter."

"What things?"

"For instance, the correct tempo of the third movement of Beethoven's Seventh Symphony."

Bill recounted how he had lost his moral virginity. It happened during his first term at Cambridge. He was shuffling back to college from lectures, scuffing his feet in the piled-up autumn leaves, and breathing the foggy air of the fens, when he looked up at the yolk of sun, which had broken into the evening sky, leaving streaks of red above the slate-grey rooftops. The world became paper-thin. He could punch his fist through Being, and it would fall apart. Reality was too fragile to sustain his weight. He fell through the veil of Maya into nothingness. He knew that all was permitted, that nothing impeded him, nothing stood in his way. He did not need to murder, rob or betray; he carried these possibilities securely within himself into the void. He would be forever alone, and solitude would also be salvation.

I listened to all that in astonished silence. The words seemed to have been broken down and re-assembled in a form that defied the rules of language. That night, Bill went on, he borrowed from his neighbour the book he had heard about in the afternoon's lecture—Eliot's *Four Quartets*.

"You don't know it, of course. You don't know that a book can be the point where past and future meet. Not because the book changes you, but because you change *it*—you read yourself into the page, and are astonished by what you find there. Listen."

Until that moment, poetry had meant nothing to me, apart from ridiculous protestations of love, descriptions of gods and heroes, and thee, thou and 'twas. But as Bill recited "Burnt Norton," I felt a kind of inner convulsion, as though the words had escaped from the normal channels of consciousness to invade the most secret, most vulnerable and most unconscious parts of my body.

Footfalls echo in the memory
Down the passage which we did not take
Towards the door we never opened
Into the rose-garden. My words echo
Thus, in your mind.
But to what purpose
Disturbing the dust on a bowl of rose-leaves
I do not know.

The words were my words, words I had lost once, had been unconsciously seeking, and had found again. And the door opened on to that mysterious rose-garden, where I was to dwell alone like Bill, and yet joined to him across an infinite distance—the distance of what might have been. From time to time as he recited I glanced at his face. It was like a mask, rigid apart from the rhythmic movement of the lips, the eyes fixed far away and the skin drawn taut across his bony features. Bill had escaped from his face into the words. He had discovered the avenue to freedom.

He finished and we did not speak. Outside, a squad of motor-scooters passed, and Bill suddenly jerked into life, turning with a rapid movement to the lace-curtained window.

"Always out there, watching, waiting!"

He said it in a whisper, but with utmost vehemence. He had begun to tremble, and to pass his hand repeatedly over his face, as though trying to free himself from the mask. In time

I was to become familiar with this crisis, yet it never ceased to disturb me. Bill was living on a knife-edge. Nothing that he valued, none of his knowledge or culture, could make him safe in the world beyond the window. The avenue to freedom that he had opened before me was one down which he could escape only in theory, and only because I was there to learn from him. Otherwise he was a prisoner—an invalid held in custody prior to the administrative decision that would settle his case.

I sat in guilty silence until the crisis passed. Then, abruptly resuming his didactic manner, Bill informed me of my ignorance of Quartets and of the astonishing thing that Beethoven had done with them. He made me drink another glass of whisky before playing the F major op. 135. I listened in amazement to the dense texture of sound, through which the instruments spoke with human voices, questioning, affirming, each one touched with the deepest inner solitude.

When I left Bill's house that evening, it was with a new conception of the world and my place in it. Henceforth nothing mattered to me save culture—which inadequate word was nevertheless the only one I had to summarize Bill's knowledge. I had entered the rose-garden, where mysterious music sounded, and the pages of a book turned slowly in a shaft of sunlight. Suburbia ended at the threshold of my being. My parents, our house and car, our TV, coffee table, and drinks cabinet, all those precise and pretty trinkets ceased to be normal and became, on the contrary, signs of a deep disorder. The real world was elsewhere, inside me, and I in it. Only through culture could you enter this world, where your eyes were always open in astonishment and your hair always on end.

We established a routine. On Wednesday evenings, when

Bill's parents were out playing whist, we would sit in the two armchairs that stood like heraldic beasts to either side of the fire-place. We would stare at the glow from the artificial coals and listen to Bill's collection of classical records. The only sounds apart from the music were the soft sipping of whisky when Bill lifted his glass from its place by his feet, and the dry scrape of his hands when he changed the record on the gramophone. He took the LPs from a pinewood cupboard behind his chair and handled the records tenderly, smoothing the translucent jackets around them before coaxing them into the sleeve. As he did so, his hands shook. I felt that, in these trembling caresses administered to a disk of black shellac, he was rehearsing a love that he would never find. How far that was from the truth, I was yet to discover.

On my free afternoons, Bill would wait for me in the garage next to the house. I would enter beneath the tip-up doors, care-fully easing them down behind me so as to make no noise. The family car was absent during weekdays, creating a space amid the suburban clutter. There, among packing cases, golf clubs, garden tools and wellington boots, stood an old chair with scuffed leather arms and a brass-buttoned back, which had been thrown out when the house was refurbished in the Swedish style, but which Bill's mother couldn't bring herself to part with, it being, as Bill put it, an offering to Hymen. He always spoke of his parents in those terms, as though their story were an archaic myth with no clear basis in reality.

In this chair, Bill would be waiting for me, his hands twisting in his lap, his face papery in the light that entered from a window on to the garden. Through this window you could see only a pair of tonsured yew trees and a white-washed wall;

they were like shapes in a modernist painting, emphasizing with their clean lines the enigma of Bill's taut expression. He would greet me with a silent stare. He did not soften this stare but merely turned away as I took up my allotted position on a packing case inside the door. Although I took care to arrive at the agreed time, he never failed to convey the impression that I was late, distracted from my duty by some trivial matter that it would be embarrassing for either of us to mention.

The sessions in the garage were arranged to coincide with my free afternoons, which were Tuesdays and Fridays. Their purpose, Bill said, was entirely educational, and my role was to listen as he expounded his vision of the world. This took the form of stories, recounting important episodes in his life from which I was free to draw whatever moral they suggested. The stories were impersonal in tone and the main protagonist—whom he referred to as Bill—had only a fleeting and inconstant resemblance to the narrator. I was told that Bill had been born and raised on an ocean-going yacht, his mother having run away with a French sailor who had been captured at Mers el-Kebir, when the French North African navy had been destroyed on Churchill's orders. This French sailor, to whom Bill gave the name Ampoule, had been held as a prisoner of war in Portsmouth until joining the free French forces as captain in a purely imaginary navy under the charge of General de Gaulle. Ampoule was not in fact Bill's father, his mother having been impregnated by a Polish airman called Marek, whom she had met in the Polish Club in London during an air-raid, and with whom she had maintained a close relationship right up until the end of the war.

Bill's birth at sea had been long-drawn out and painful, and his mother would have died in child-birth had it not been for a passing ocean liner that stopped in answer to Ampoule's distress call, and hoisted the mother on board. I should say, Bill went on, that Bill's mother is not the woman you see padding along the corridors of this house, polishing the brass, straightening the furniture and stacking the *Reader's Digest* books beneath the television. That woman assumed charge of Bill during his early years, after his real mother had died in an accident on a model railway in Whipsnade zoo. Nor need I add that Bill's father, no trace of whom remains, has no connection with that woman's husband, whom she married in an ordinary ceremony in a registry office in Croydon, some months before receiving Bill into her keeping. But what a start in life, if ever there was one!

His real mother loved him, of that Bill was sure when he lost sight of her forever aged 3; and he is still sure of it. It is from her that Bill acquired his love of poetry and music, and often in the dead of night, when he starts awake and his eyes see lights on the far horizon, he hears her calling to him, hears again the soft voice with which she had soothed his infant nightmares, smells again the cheap talc which she always wore, a large box of which had been stolen for her use by Marek when he was working at the camp for Polish airmen, a box which he had handed to her with ceremonial Polish chivalry the day before he committed suicide by jumping under a goods train. Often in the early years, before they had tamed him and compelled him to a life of study, Bill would wander far from home, always sensing her voice, guiding him, encouraging him, speaking to him of a love that would never be removed from him since it depended on no mortal circumstance, but lay buried beneath his life, like a treasure that drew him to a secret place that had been set apart for him, and where one day he would enter and be at home.

Meanwhile, however, there were the dull routines of exile. This is what they hadn't understood, Bill's guardians and tormentors. They hadn't understood that he did not belong in the place where they had confined him, and that there was no need to summon the police, as they invariably did, when his bedroom was found empty in the morning, and his rucksack absent from the coat-stand in the downstairs corridor. The main purpose of these adventures was to explore the modern world as it was, to obtain a spiritual map of the place that God had only recently abandoned, and to compose a book of instructions for future travellers. Oh yes, the world will be grateful one day for Bill, when the guide-book has been committed to paper. And you, Michael, will be grateful to have it from Bill's lips.

The adventures began when Bill was a teenager. Until that moment, he had kept his mission to himself, lived in exile among the Giants without challenging their ludicrous stories, including the story that he was their son and the heir to their stupidities. It was in the early hours of a damp, misty morning in the summer of 1967 that he left on the first stage of his mission. He went by bus and train to London, lodged in a hostel for the homeless in Mile End, and began to patrol the streets of the great metropolis in search of shadows. Those shadows were everywhere in T.S. Eliot's day, and the first thing Bill discovered was that *The Waste Land* described a world that had disappeared. Here and there, it is true, he came across a shadow, blown across his path like a scrap of paper bearing some enigmatic message. But for the most part, he walked in a light that hurt his eyes and his mind. The bright windows of shops and restaurants, the radiant aisles of the bombed-out churches, the hurrying streets of the city and the green crescents of Notting Hill—all stood in a light that rained down on them from the future, a future to which Bill could never belong. He made friends with a tramp, an expert on the writings of James Joyce, and together they studied *Ulysses*, in which a real city is allegedly described, full of the real people that make cities possible. Bill was not taken in. He understood at once that Joyce's Dublin is a place more dreamed than lived, that the realities have been carefully concealed behind the images, and that Joyce's art is an art of subterfuge, a way of cheating one's way to the thought that life goes on.

But life does not go on. That was what Bill learned in London, and if it had not been for the fact of his arrest one night on suspicion of stealing the plaster-cast mermaid that had vanished from the foyer of the seamen's hostel where the tramp had found a temporary lodging, he would have taken the train north to Scotland, to pursue his mission there. As it was, he found himself back in the routine devised by the Giants, forced to postpone his plans for the future, and to resume his pretended life as an obedient moron.

In his imagined wanderings, Bill fell in with characters burdened with information fundamental to his education and to mine. There was the constructivist architect Miastotkin, who had unfurled for Bill's instruction—and my instruction too—his plans for the total destruction of London. There was the composer of musicals and seaside medleys, Harry Bile, whose settings of William Blake had been chosen to open the Chelsea Flower Show two years before. There was Mick, the rag and bone man, Auntie the acrobat and Sam Hibbard in his flasher's mackintosh, who had taught the art of growing vegetables on an allotment under the railway. From all of these I learned—politics, philosophy, music, modern history, topics bundled together by Bill as 'the arts of survival'. And there was Father Ryszard, the Polish priest, who had been a ground officer with bomber command in the Second World War. Father Ryszard's stories, of Poland under communism, of Nazi criminals hidden at that very moment in our suburb, were related with an urgency and conviction that quite belied their implausibility.

"I returned to Poland," Father Ryszard had said one night (he and Bill were working as ice-cream vendors in Birmingham at the time) "at just the wrong moment after the war, when the communists were hunting down the patriots who had fought the Nazis and the ruined country was being wrapped in human skin as a gift for Comrade Stalin. I had no thought then of entering the priesthood, could hardly say that I was a believer, and spent my spare time chasing girls, as we all did. It was a few weeks after VE day that I underwent a change of heart. I was stationed then in an old-fashioned market town where wizened old geezers made furniture from the local beech trees, and quaint traditions like Morris dancing and maypoles were maintained as symbols of England's right to exist. There was a camp on a neighbouring hillside where the Polish airmen were housed, and by way of ministering to our manifest moral deficiencies we had been provided with a Roman Catholic priest, a sad old man called Father Brendan Murphy, who had been brought over from Ireland for the purpose, following his retirement from a country parish. Father Brendan was a heavy drinker, who would spend his evenings in the Coach and Horses Inn, presiding, with the help of his flock, over a constant flow of beer and Irish whiskey. Towards ten o'clock, as the pub emptied and the next day's agenda dawned on those unfortunate enough to have one, Father Brendan would begin to talk, often interrupting himself with astonished cries as the visions revealed themselves, usually on the opposite wall, but once in the face of Millie, the bar-maid, for whom he had a tender affection. It was these visions that were my downfall. For after a while I began to share in them. 'See there,' Father Brendan would cry, 'the Holy Virgin herself, sorting her knitting needles'; or 'You wouldn't believe it, the Angel Gabriel himself talking to Jan Kowalski there; as though it could do any good. And what's that in his hand? An electric saw? Good Heavens.'

"At first the visions were random in just that way, odd intrusions of the miraculous that served no purpose other than to cast doubt on the reality of our surroundings. Gradually, though, they took on a distinct narrative form, and it was in this way that they sucked me in. The Holy Virgin ceased to fuss around with knitting and darning and baking cakes, and began to make definite pronouncements about the way the world was going. 'Listen,' Father Brendan would say, firmly gripping my arm, 'she is telling us about the war in Japan.' And sure enough, into the silence that followed—for it was late and we were alone in the corner of the saloon bar—there intruded a soft female voice, speaking Polish. But it was not about Japan that she was speaking. She murmured for a while, soothing nonsense of a vaguely religious kind. And then she mentioned the village of Podgorze, my village, and the plight of my mother who had no one to protect her since my father's death from tuberculosis two years before. I began to reason with her—how could I go home now, when my status in the British air force would be a death sentence in the Communists' eyes? I proved irrefutably that I was of the greatest use to mankind and to the church as a member of the ground staff of Bomber Command, and Father Brendan, for whom I purchased a double whiskey as an encouragement, pleaded the case on my behalf.

"But the Holy Virgin was having none of it. She intimated that I was to return to Poland in the guise of a Roman Catholic priest, and as it happens the vestments and rings and chasubles were all to hand and already lodged with Father Brendan who would lend them to me forthwith, which he did, gladly exchanging his clothing for mine and disappearing thereafter from the camp where we were housed and leaving me to improvise my new identity as best I could."

You will ask whether Bill believed this story of Father Ryszard's, and the answer is of course that he didn't, and that in any case it did not matter since at that moment two police officers had approached the ice-cream van that Father Ryszard had borrowed from a neighbour and arrested him as an illegal immigrant. It was only later, while rehearsing a play by Ionesco for the *Théatre du cornichon* in the Latin quarter, that he had time to reflect on the meaning of Father Ryszard and the significance, not for Bill and me only, but for Europe as a whole, of the mad Polish resistance to communism. And here, leaving everything once again in the air, Bill took the opportunity to explain to me the real meaning of Ionesco's surrealist theatre as he saw it, the place of surrealism in the literature of post-war Paris, and the significance of the theatre in enabling the French to express their guilt feelings about the war, without ever making them so clear as to amount to a real confession. From this topic, it was but a small step to the existentialism of Jean-Paul Sartre and the theory of the *pour-soi* as the *néant*.

I owe my education almost entirely to Bill. His Scheherazade-like stories, which never concluded but opened brackets within brackets in a constant flow of information, were designed to create between us a relation of tense complicity, as the only ones in the know. I was to share his secret vision, which was a vision of time and its meaning, a vision of the catastrophe of the modern world, in which nevertheless there was rescue available if only I would entrust myself to him. His stories described the possible worlds in which Bill existed just as he is, but somehow purified, real but washed clean of the facts. They were illustrations of those lines in his favourite poem, which tell us that "What might have been and what has been / Point to one end, which is always present." Bill became a symbol of the present: a vivid shining of the Now, which seemed like a candle burning with all the past Nows of our civilization, and made from human tallow. Although the twisted figure in the scuffed old armchair could easily be mistaken for an abject failure, the appearance was entirely deceptive—such was the burden of his words. Beneath the broken-seeming exterior was a vital and creative soul, and soon that soul would burst from its ruined chrysalis and take me with it into the skies. All that was necessary was patience. I had to trust him, in some way to give myself to him, and I sat in my corner of the garage dimly apprehensive as to what my commitment to Bill amounted to and what price I would soon be called upon to pay.

Bill lent me books: Eliot, Joyce, and Beckett; Goethe, Heine, and Rilke; Flaubert, Baudelaire, and Maupassant. He played through his collection of records, and soon the love of Beethoven and Mahler had displaced all lesser loves—I knew that I must study music. There was an old upright piano in our house, the legacy of an aunt who had died. I began to work out melodies and chords, and to teach myself the rudiments of theory. Bill told me he could play a little, and I asked him to give me a lesson on our old piano. He greeted the suggestion with horror.

"Impossible," he said. "Not there. *This* is where I live. On a temporary basis, you understand, but live nevertheless."

I bullied my parents, and they agreed to pay for lessons, which I received from old Dr. Jackson, the organist at the Anglican church. Within three months I had my fingers under control and was teaching myself to sight-read, devouring volume after volume from the public library, whose unvisited music section contained all the classics in out-of-date editions. Bill was gratified by my progress, though he never heard me play, there being no piano within the ambit of his permitted excursions. For six months, we would meet at his house on bridge nights, or in his garage on my school-free afternoons. Along with his autobiographical stories, he would entertain me with descriptions of my ignorance, and parsimonious hints as to how I might be cured of it. Soon I had the impression that he was indeed winding me into the fiction in which he lived. I was no longer Michael Sillitoe, but 'Michael Sillitoe', a character in a story by Bill.

During the summer holidays, we would often spend the days together reading his "curriculum for castaways," and I wrote one or two essays, which I did not dare to show to him, but which pleased me with their posturing sensitivity to things half understood. By the time I returned to school in September to prepare for the Cambridge entrance examination, I had begun to adopt his cryptic dialect.

I had discovered in the town library a strange little periodical called *Die Reihe,* edited by Ernst Křenek, one of those difficult and impossibly intellectual composers who emerged from the Viennese twilight with dictatorial imperatives directed at the rest of mankind. The journal was considered so important by the cognoscenti that it appeared simultaneously in German and English. It told me that the classical tradition of music had come to an end, that tonality had reached a crisis, and that the language of music must be forged anew. I asked Bill what this could possibly mean, and he explained, standing with his back to the lace-curtained window and conducting himself with vast waves of the arms.

"All art must renew itself. To repeat the old gestures, the old styles, the old devices, is to lapse into cliché. What was once fresh and full of meaning becomes dead and empty like a shell."

"So you think the musical tradition is finished?"

"Tradition is the slant of things, leaning against the wind. It doesn't cease just because the dead leaves are blown away."

"You're avoiding the question," I said.

"No. I am rephrasing it. Listen."

And he put a record on the turntable. It was the last movement of Mahler's ninth symphony—a piece so sublime, to my way of thinking, that I felt the existence of an absolute divide between those who had heard it and those who had not, like the absolute divide between the saved and the damned. I was all the more astonished by Bill's words, which he delivered in a vehement whisper above the great G-string melody for the first violins.

"Listen to that turn—the way it lingers around the single note, dwelling on its putrefaction. Horrible! Horrible! And here it comes again, caressing the dead, necrophilia in music, and this dead thing a child! Someone else's child—stolen as a sacrificial victim."

Suddenly he snatched the needle from the record.

"Of course it wasn't always like that. The turn was a beautiful ornament in Bach, a delicate piece of stitching in Mozart, a source of boundless energy in the first movement of the Emperor concerto. And then came Wagner, and a premonition of twilight. The Liebestod—the first welcoming of death in music—and the farewell to the old musical language."

I confessed that I had not heard the Liebestod, and Bill turned to stare at me, as though noticing my presence for the first time.

"Tomorrow you will not be going to school," he said. "We shall sit here and listen through *Tristan*. And since you read music, we shall follow it with the score."

Bill swept the room with his eyes.

"You need to know what is really wrong with this place and time. You need to know how much is fake."

For the first time, I bridled against Bill's regime of absolutes. Was it my fault that I had been reared in ignorance? I looked at him angrily, and he instantly lowered his eyes.

"I know. You've got to live. Why should you see things my way? Look at old Bill, you're thinking—a prisoner, an invalid, a moral cripple. And he tells me everything else is fake."

I was distressed by these words. It had not occurred to me to doubt Bill's vision—on the contrary, every day left me more persuaded of its truth. Bill was an invalid, but only in the way that soldiers might be invalids. He had done battle with the world and been honourably wounded. And he had seized from the world its secrets, which he was sharing with me.

"I do see things your way, Bill. It's why I've changed. Just don't expect more than is possible, that's all."

The next day I played truant from school—it wasn't difficult, since I had finished my A-levels, and was left to my own devices, on the assumption that my devices had the same goal as the school's, namely Cambridge. But I didn't go immediately to Bill's. Something was on my mind—something that I couldn't put into words. Three years before, I had been confirmed in the Church of England; our family assumed that, once you got into the right position, this was a useful move, like castling in chess. It relieved you of the need to go to church, much as becoming a shareholder relieved you of the need to work for the firm. It also put God permanently on your side. For a brief moment, I had been moved by the Anglican rite, and I suppose the Book of Common Prayer must have penetrated my unconscious thoughts—whence came that sudden and devastating sense of recognition on hearing *Four Quartets,* if not from the memory of Cranmer? Some of this had come back during my lessons with Dr. Jackson, who had a touching love for the old hymns and chants and words, and who never failed to remind me that the music of Bach, which we studied together, was written in praise of our Saviour.

Interesting people were rare in our part of the world, and you encountered them only by chance. Our clubs and societies were designed to endow brainless hobbies with an aura of neighbourliness; people with visions of the higher life had to nourish them in private. Their situation was not desperate, for the Third Programme provided lectures, plays, poetry, and high-minded comment, along with serious music. And I suppose we were all to some extent creations of the old BBC—even Bill, whose contempt for the world echoed the patrician attitudes that floated on the air-waves. Nevertheless, you could not encounter a cultivated person without a feeling of complicity, of mutual secrets, and a shared but unspecified danger. There was a freemasonry of the elect, and even if you never overtly mentioned it, this very fact conditioned what you said or did together. So it was with Dr. Jackson, into whose book-lined cottage in the old part of town I would make my way each Wednesday evening, to subject my musical skills to judgement.

Dr. Jackson was in his early fifties, a quiet bachelor who had been an organ scholar at an Oxford college. Failing to obtain a fellowship, he had returned to his mother's house, bringing the books, records, and beliefs acquired at Oxford. His mother died, and thereafter he lived by teaching the piano to the half a dozen kids whose parents saw the point of it. A frugal lifestyle and studious piety had endowed his features with an air of saintliness. The mild grey eyes never stared or demanded, but looked always shyly upwards from beneath a rose-coloured brow, on which a crown of white hair shone like a halo. The long straight mouth was sheltered behind a salt-and-pepper moustache, and would venture a smile before every utterance. Dr. Jackson dressed correctly, in worn-out tweeds, with a gold watch tucked in his waistcoat, and a green silk handkerchief, which he never used, carefully arranged in his top pocket. He was quietly spoken, and his words were punctuated with long, thoughtful silences, as though he feared to speak out of turn, and was waiting for a sign. To me he was always gracious, never explicitly mentioning, but merely assuming, that I shared his musical passions. He had a curious way of inserting information sideways into your mind—not stating what he wished you to know, but merely prompting you to recall it.

"Makes you uncomfortable, doesn't it, the A flat in the bass, straight after the F sharp in the bar before." (He was going through the first prelude in the Forty-Eight, note by note as he always did.) "Of course you're familiar with the controversy, whether there isn't a bar missing—Czerny gives us one, with G in the bass and a C minor arpeggio above, but you wouldn't want that, I dare say, being much more of a modernist than poor old Czerny." (After a long pause, listening to my swallowed silence, he would continue.) "It probably sounds mad to you, but I like to compare that A flat with the C sharp in the first theme of the Eroica—the note from elsewhere. Watch out, it says, music is full of surprises—you think you're on firm ground and—Good Heavens!—you've stepped on a trap door and are falling through keys you never dreamed of."

And he would conclude with a self-deprecating chuckle. From such lessons I would go straight to the town library, in order to discover for myself what Dr. Jackson had revealed through pretending that I already knew it. Nor were his asides about music only. To each of Bach's fugal subjects he gave a name from Shakespeare: the C minor in Book I was Malvolio, the C-sharp major Portia, the E-flat minor Cordelia, and so on. And by assuming that I knew exactly what he meant, he led me in the most original way to read and remember Shakespeare, and to acknowledge as I did so the profound oneness of the artistic enterprise, which, whether in words or tones or paint, was always exalting our condition and redeeming it.

The modern world seemed not to have touched the little close beside the church where Dr. Jackson's cottage stood amid flagstones and roses. There was neither telephone nor television in his living room, and the worn oriental carpets and antique furniture had an air of unassuming gentility, like the much-loved remnants of a family used to living in far grander places, but now in decline. The genial antiquity of his surroundings was reflected in his manner, and although I admired Bill's livid truthfulness, I could not help noticing the fact that a person could be as cultured as Bill and yet serene and reconciled. And Dr. Jackson did not hide the cause of his contentment. On the contrary, by assuming Christian faith, he also conveyed it—not as a proselytising doctrine, but as the atmosphere in which he lived and breathed.

Although he did not care for modernists, Dr. Jackson had a rooted love of the art and music that had been modern in his youth—especially of the paintings of Paul Nash and the music of Vaughan Williams. He drew my attention to these things in his usual way, by assuming that I knew them, and referred, shyly but approvingly, to their roots in the landscape. Gradually I acquired from Dr. Jackson something that had no place either in the life of our suburb or in the mind of Bill, which was an idea of England, as a spiritual rather than a geographical location. Into this spiritual niche were slotted, like votive offerings at a shrine, the worn and treasured icons of our spent tradition: the Anglican Church, with its hymns and prayers and liturgies; landscape painting and pastoral music; and the poems and novels of the great Victorians, three of whom—Hardy, Housman, and Hopkins—had a special meaning for him on account of their valedictory sadness. When I entered Dr Jackson's cottage, and took my place at the old Chappell grand to which he beckoned me with a shy, gentle wave of the hand, I would recall those words from *Four Quartets:* "History is now and England," and feel growing in some secret part of me shoots sent out from ancestors long buried and decomposed.

This feeling had taken a new turn, just in the weeks before Bill decided that I must be initiated into *Tristan*. The cause of this was my first girlfriend, daughter of a bank-manager, whom I had met at an organ recital given by Dr. Jackson in the church. The pews in front of me were empty, although the concert was due to begin. I turned to look at the organ loft, hoping to give a sign of encouragement to Dr. Jackson, and found my eyes captured by a girl in a cream-coloured mackintosh and a loose sky-blue scarf, who sat alone in the pews three rows behind me. She was tall, pretty, with high pale cheeks, primrose-coloured hair and blue eyes that looked from far away. I smiled at her and she smiled back. Thanks to Dr. Jackson I had a few opening gambits. The concert over, I thought it best to go straight for the kill, like Ferdinand in *The Tempest*: "my prime request / Which I do last pronounce, is, O you wonder! / If you be maid or no?"

She gave her own version of Miranda, with "No wonder Sir, but certainly made for adventure." Nothing could have been further from the truth. Linda belonged in the normal world, as did I. We walked through the town to her suburban street—like ours except the houses were bigger, with shrub-filled gardens, plane trees, and at the end, bordering the open country, the biggest house of all, which belonged to her parents. She had come down for the summer holidays from a minor public school, and welcomed my attentions, perhaps because they came from someone who could never be "the boyfriend." When we reached the drive to the posh gabled house that claimed her, she turned with a brief goodbye, which was not especially encouraging. But I was grateful, since I had learned where she lived, and was keen to experiment with my first love-letter, confident that the way to her heart was through writing. These were the seventies, remember. The class system was still in force, and boys from grammar schools were regarded by girls from public schools with a lofty disdain that could be overcome only by talent and bravado.

Actually Linda was drawn to me—not in a big way, but quietly. She replied to my letter by return, and with heart-stopping candour. She liked music up to a point—the point where it became serious. She had read a few books, was considering becoming an intellectual, and was shortly to go up to Oxford to study French. We should be friends, she wrote, and then see what came of it.

I soon discovered that music and literature were of questionable significance to her. Far more important was the Christian religion. She had been brought up and confirmed in the Anglican Church. But religion had happened later, in the form of a vision. She was preparing for bed one evening—it was the Easter holidays, she had just returned in high spirits to the sunny house at the end of Condale Close, her two older brothers were playing billiards in the room below, the exhilarating comforts of childhood were spread around—when an angel appeared. She was forbidden to see him, except from the corner of her eye; but he spoke to her, and as he spoke she glimpsed through the golden radiance an astonishing expanse of nakedness. His words were obscure, and although she tried hard to concentrate, she understood only that she must pray in church and live in charity towards those less fortunate than herself—which meant just about everybody. The angel vanished, and she lay on her bed in tears of joy.

Of course, the immediate effect of this vision had worn off by the time I met Linda, who was, as I said, a more or less normal suburban eighteen-year-old, apart from her habit of praying in church and visiting old ladies on their death-beds. But it had fortified her music-hall virginity. Philip Larkin was wrong. Sex hadn't begun in our suburb even in 1975, though rumours were rife. Linda's kisses were fresh, eager, and yet abruptly curtailed at the moment of passion. They tasted of sea-side and tea-time and were about as daring as a sneaked cigarette. Nevertheless, they made a hole in my emotions that took a long time to fill. Thanks to Linda I sometimes went to church, to sit among the sparse and ageing population, watching her slender form as she stepped sedate and joyful like a bride towards the altar. During the communion Dr. Jackson would improvise on the stopped diapason, around squishy chords lifted from the English water-cress school—Finzi, Warlock, and John Ireland trickled into the depths of my being, and made there a pool of unshed tears.

I had not told Bill of my feelings for Linda, nor of my interest in the church. Beside the absolute and ascetic standard that he set, they both seemed disreputable. I had come across references to Wagner's *Tristan,* so I knew that it dealt with sexual love. But I was appalled at the thought of discussing such a thing with Bill. Astonished as I had been to discover that I was normal in that department, I could not believe such a thing of Bill. He had been blown by an inner explosion high above the realm of human contact, and was perched on the branch of some blighted oak-tree, forever immune to temptation, watching and disdaining all.

I spent that morning alone, taking a bus to the village of Etticombe, which stood on a tree-covered rise above quilted pasture-land, a Disneyland model of old England on the doorstep of the London sprawl. It was a cloudless day, with a slight breath of autumn, soon warmed away by the sun. I sat beneath an ancient yew in the churchyard, idly surveying the graves of people who had died in ages when the good died young, and the bad survived them by a year or two. I listened to wrens and warblers, to the sounds of insects about their late summer business, and to the hourly strokes of a cracked old bell in the lichen-covered tower of stone behind me. I watched old ladies come and go in their flowery dresses, and exchanged courtesies across a fence with an ageing shire horse. I read from a book of Hardy's poems; every now and then my thoughts would turn to Linda, and a deep delicious melancholy would invade me—a yearning for vanished things, and for a purity that was mocked by the world.

Bill, I knew, would never have countenanced such feelings. He recognized only one mortal sin, which was sentimentality—the pretended love of useful fictions. He justified his indifference to politics in this way. The nationalist dreams of Enoch Powell, the Labour Party's icon of the working class, the high-flown rhetoric of the Trades Union Congress, and the loyal toasts of the Tories: in each of them he discerned the same disqualifying stigma. All were riddled with sentimental pretence, and Bill would dismiss any reference to them with an angry wave of the hand. For me, however, they had begun to acquire a coating of antique gold. They were bits of the great jigsaw puzzle of England. I was beginning to put the puzzle together, from those small but potent clues that Dr. Jackson and Linda, in their different ways, provided. I had come across Ruskin and William Morris, and felt drawn to a kind of Christianised socialism that endowed even the Labour Government of Mr. Wilson with an air of ancestral legitimacy. Three years later, when I had left for Cambridge, and the grammar school to which I owed my chances was destroyed, I began to have my doubts about socialism. But by then I had withdrawn from the world, and was as remote from politics as Bill.

It was not politics that focussed my thoughts on that morning. For several weeks the dual force of Dr. Jackson and Linda had worked inextricably on my emotions, in a way that I can only describe as "pastoral." Around, above, and beneath me I sensed the presence of the believing dead, to whom I was tied by a religion that I had never adopted but which I could not discard. In the little church at Etticombe, with its smell of damp plaster, late summer roses, and polished brass, its pews hung with embroidered knee rests, and its altar neatly decked with wildflowers, I could feel the power of Eliot's lines:

You are not here to verify,
Instruct yourself, or inform curiosity
Or carry report. You are here to kneel
Where prayer has been valid.

And I wanted, in a curious way, to understand and accept that potent "has been." I wanted to *pass through* the Anglican faith, to understand its living history, to accept and tolerate and then reject it, not with an oafish gesture of dismissal, but sadly and lingeringly, as one says farewell to an ailing parent before crossing the seas. And this curious desire was mingled in my imagination with the fresh smell of Linda's face, with the modal harmonies of English music, and with the quiet nave of Etticombe church, where the light slid down on dusty beams to lie in pools on the floor.

To purge these useless feelings it would have been enough to take a bus-journey in the opposite direction, to the new shopping centre on the by-pass, to the streets of Croydon which ran like roaring gullies between sheer-faced office-blocks, to the endless, senseless, lifeless miles of houses just like ours. But first love is selective, and my first love was neither Linda nor Bill nor Dr. Jackson, but England—not the England of suburbs, TV dinners, and motorways, but the great spiritual fact whose outline I tried to guess from the fragments I had assembled, and which could be glimpsed from time to time like Linda's angel, out of the corner of your eye, and in these special places where history flickers for a moment like a guttering candle.

I took the afternoon bus back to our suburb in a state of calm exaltation. I had formed the intention—quite crazy in the circumstances, but arising with a kind of logic from my elegy in a country churchyard—to marry Linda. Not yet, of course, not immediately. But some time in the not too distant future, when we had been through university, and I had become a famous writer or composer or something of the sort, and she had matured to the point of seeing that nothing less than that would do. I had earmarked a property in Etticombe, a brick and timber cottage with a thatched roof and a "for sale" notice jabbed into the greensward outside. Into this toy-town bower I planned to lead her, to live cut off from the world but nevertheless together, with the same pure habits as Dr. Jackson, only with thoughts and feelings wilder than the wildest of Bill's. All that remained was to gain Linda's consent, and with that end in view I made at once for the house in Condale Close—to which, by the way, I had never been invited—not wishing to diminish my resolve with anything so vulgar as a phone call.

Linda herself came to the door, dressed in a forget-me-not blouse and white trousers, telephone in one hand, receiver in the other, the cord trailing from polished and wax-scented darkness. She looked at me as though I were a visitor from the Gestapo, and then stepped quickly backwards, holding her hand over the mouthpiece and saying "wait a moment." I stood on the doorstep, and heard her say in urgent tones that she could not talk and would explain everything later. And then she came out to me, her face troubled and annoyed. I tried to hold on to my great decision, but it fled like a dream before the daylight, and I followed her in silence as she headed past me for the street.

"What's up?" she said at last.

"Oh, I've been thinking, that's all."

What was the use of culture, when it could provide no better words than those?

"What exactly?"

Linda's breeding was expressed in everything she said and did. As she strode on her long legs towards our usual footpath, which ambled beside cornfields to suburban streets like hers, she was setting the pace for me, physically, emotionally, and morally. I could see in her bothered features how small a consideration she could afford to me, how much the idea of a good marriage to a conventional man had been tacitly assumed in all her dealings, and how little hope I had of deflecting her from the course that had been instilled from birth. I answered her question, but in a small, dispirited voice that was bound to repel her.

"I've been thinking that we can't just go on, seeing each other, doing things together, and all that. I mean, we should consider the future."

She shot a bright sudden glance in my direction.

"I've been thinking the same," she said.

The expression of annoyance had disappeared, and she

strode with a remote smile on her lips, a smile that was not for me. We were not in the habit of touching; nevertheless, I could sense that she was taking special care to avoid my hand as it swung beside her.

"So how do you see things?" I asked.

"Me? I think we should just be friends. I'm off to Oxford, you will be another term at least at school, and we don't want any difficulties."

"So there's someone else," I said. It was not that I drew this conclusion; on the contrary, I was rapidly assessing the evidence with a view to refuting it. But I had seen a way to dramatize my predicament. The pathos of faithful love in the face of rejection was sure to move her, just as it moved me, who had invented the role. I would stir the waters of her being with my wounded devotion, and those clear blue eyes would be troubled for me. This role-playing was supposed to be the final proof of love. Linda was not one to fall for it.

"There's always someone else."

"Not in my case," I said proudly.

"There's always going to be, until the crucial point, when the mind is made up."

"Well, that's what I'm saying. I've reached that point. My mind is made up."

I hesitated, shifting words about in my thoughts, suddenly aware of the ridiculous sound of "marriage" on the lips of a seventeen-year old. From the calm breeze-stroked landscape of my imagined England, the slender transparency of Linda was suddenly deleted.

"Then that makes two of us," she said.

And it seemed better to me, too, that this attempt at love

had failed. I could nurse my sadness and my jealousy, and press them into the roots of my being. My all-pervasive sense of loss now had a personal meaning.

It was mid-afternoon when I parted from Linda, she walking briskly towards the town, no doubt to offer a prayer of gratitude, I limping homewards. Tears, such as they were, had dried on my cheeks long before I passed Bill's house, and when I saw him standing in the window, and realized that his parents would not yet be home, I decided to visit him. As I walked up the gravel path to the front door, he watched me with an air of astonishment, as though I were returning from the dead. It was a long time before he came to the door.

"To look at people and doubt that they are apes," he said; "even here, in this shit-house—how is it possible?"

It was not a promising start.

"Sorry I didn't make it for *Tristan*," I said, as matter-of-factly as I could. "I had a few problems."

He laughed his soft, sad, humourless laugh and walked back into the house. I followed uninvited, and watched him beating the air in the living room, not looking at me, but chuckling to himself and addressing the furniture with lunatic stares. Maybe I didn't need such a sight, but it held me riveted. Bill's crises had the appearance of a victory for mind over matter—mind long-suffering and cruelly imprisoned, bursting asunder the fetters of flesh. In fact they were the opposite, but that was something that I understood only much later.

"What are you doing to me, Michael?"

The words shocked and frightened me. In all my dealings with Bill, it had never occurred to me that he could feel anything towards me, other than a desire to pass on his knowledge.

"Like I said, I'm sorry."

"Yes, but you're happy. You've got everything you want, me included."

"Happy?" I said. "What on earth do you mean?"

I was out of my depth here, and a storm was breaking on the near horizon.

"Happiness means looking in the mirror and not taking fright," Bill said. "It is also an extremely vulgar condition, which you should study to avoid."

"But I do avoid it. Today, for instance, I threw away my chances with the only girl I... the only... well, with my girlfriend sort of."

"With my girlfriend sort of," Bill said mockingly. "I knew it. The same old disease. Girlfriend!"

I tried to feel offended, but Bill became suddenly pitiable in his loneliness, moving with ever slower steps around the room, shielding his head with his hands, and bowing beneath the thing that pecked at his shining cranium. I wanted to explain about my elegiac grief, which would surely demonstrate that I stood side by side with him in the scheme of things. But I had no words, and stood mutely amid the hideous furnishings like a new arrival at a dog's home. Bill's gyrations ceased entirely, and with a sigh, he fell face down on to the sofa, and slid to his knees on the floor.

For minutes he did not move. I watched a pair of crows, as they pursued each other from tree to tree in the roadway. Jealous fantasies were roused by their raucous cries: Linda's kisses, no longer innocent, but lapped up like gravy by hearty young men. The pain grew until, almost unbearable, it suddenly burst and dissolved. In its place came an anxious desolation, as I surveyed the changeless changing of the street outside, and thought of the moments stretching to infinity and the arrow of the present forever lodged in my brain. Without warning Bill jumped to his feet and began speaking in a rapid voice, like a machine gun.

"O.K. so you like girls Michael Sillitoe, you are normal and natural and bourgeois and boring and a credit to your parents. You have decided to humour your ascetic neighbour, and squeeze culture out of him like juice from an orange, since girls like culture and, within reasonable limits, parents don't mind it either. And of course it helps that your neighbour is a freak fit for nothing except to stand vigil at the grave of art and wait for the resurrection. And then, of course, you'll be off to Cambridge to equip yourself with a degree in science and old Bill will be forgotten."

There was much more in that vein before he collapsed on the sofa in tears. I stared at Bill in the way one stares at accidents and insects. I didn't know much about life. But I knew that if I did not deny Linda, it was all over with Bill, and that it would soon be all over with Bill in any case. I decided to deny Linda. I wanted to play for time, before returning to my galaxy. I told him that I was as much an ascetic as he was, that I had been interested in Linda, but only for cultural reasons, and on account of this vision of England that had been troubling me. And as I fumbled my way through those elegiac emotions, expecting geysers of mockery to erupt at any moment from his shining skull-cap, I remembered Linda's kisses, and the clear, fresh promise of a redemption that was something higher and finer than anything that could be said in words. Bill did not mock. Instead he stared at me with growing horror, and at last held his hands to his ears.

"Stop, stop," he said, "this can't go on. England, shmingland, you sound like the Archers. Where did you pick up that stuff? Certainly not from me. Listen, let me tell you something. T.S. Eliot was an American, brought up on German philosophy. He couldn't care a fuck about England, the real England I mean, and might as well have lived on another planet. His religion was as phony as yours is, and everything that's good in his poetry came from Mallarmé and Baudelaire and Laforgue."

The anger in Bill's voice was directed not to what I had said, but to what I had not said. He was beating Linda into oblivion, driving her from the sphere of our friendship. And I saw with a terrible apprehension that Bill had no other resource. He had stood for months at the window of his parents' house, hoping to be offered a reason for existing. One day I passed, and he saw that I was that reason. Since then he had emptied at my feet his store of knowledge. As the conflagration raced through my mind, I understood why I could not discuss love and sex with Bill. Something would become explicit which must be concealed.

Bill ranted for a while about T.S. Eliot, went to put a record on the turntable, thought better of it, poured a slug of whisky down his throat, coughed, ranted again, and at last stood in a state of shaking dereliction by the window, wrapping himself in the mustard-yellow curtains, and staring crazily at the Victorian milkmaid whose figure formed the pattern in the wallpaper. The real loss, I understood, is the loss of that which you never possessed—like my loss of Linda, and Bill's loss of me. The sight of his need disturbed me, and I wanted to run from the house and be alone—maybe forever. But that which disturbed me also transfixed me.

Bill began speaking again, this time quietly, tonelessly, so that I had to strain to catch his words.

"There's one thing you've got to realize Michael, which is that our world wasn't made in England. Nothing remains of England, except the mockery that you see from this window. The England of Gray's *Elegy* is no more real than the England of Wordsworth or Dickens or George Eliot: it has been swept away with the Empire and the aristocracy and the great lake of illusions which was the Anglican church. All that remains is a pack of Christmas cards. Our world—the one where you and I exist, and maybe no one else at all, certainly no one else for miles and miles around—that world was made in Germany. It was made by Bach and Beethoven and Brahms and Wagner. It was made by Kant and Hegel and Fichte and Schopenhauer. It was made by Goethe and Schiller and Rilke and Thomas Mann. We are boxed-in romantics, and we have painted our world on the walls of our prison. German culture provided our themes: it showed us how to rejoice in loneliness, it showed us how to look down on normal life and plant thought-bombs on its highways. That is how we—you and I, that is—survive. But down there, where the others live, great heaps of junk are building up, the debris of a dead civilization. In fact, should you even call it a civilization?"

Bill looked at me suddenly. Of a certainty he was not giving me a tutorial about German culture. He was trying to warn me, but against what?

"There is a book that I should like you to avoid. It is called *The Decline of the West*. You will not have heard of it, and you are to behave as though it did not exist. The geezer who wrote it was a German too, and a romantic, who believed that he was living at the end of things, that nothing lay before him save a desert of hilarious trivia, a kind of cultural moonscape trampled by orange-trousered morons eating candy-floss. If you think that you go mad. You've got to decamp to a private world. You've got to fill the space of your solitude with pure and beautiful things. You've got to live in memory and alienation and *Sehnsucht*. And you've got to turn your monk's eyes on the crowd and see through them as though they were air."

His soft laugh had returned, and as he spoke he slowly and carefully worked himself free from the curtain, as though unwrapping a gift. In the light from the window his skin was stretched and powdery, and his head was a hollow skull. His words were like a testament, and I sensed that he would soon be dead. I held myself taut as he came across to me. His lips on my cheek were cold, dry and motionless, and he trembled slightly as he stroked my arm.

"The Giants will be home in a moment," he said. "Come tomorrow evening. They'll be playing whist. We'll listen to *Tristan.*"

I did not sleep that night. Bill's deathly kiss lingered for hours, burning a hole in my cheek, seeking the enduring bone in me. Under its spell I became a *memento mori*, and the thought of Bill holding and kissing my skull filled me with horror. Linda would have made me whole and safe. But Linda was gone. Nothing stood between me and disaster save my own will, and my will needed a bit more of a supporting cast than was currently available.

I began to marshal the arguments against Bill, and of course there were many. He had been urging me to break with everything, to be an outsider, sleeping rough somewhere in a hammock, while plotting the end of the world. Yet his own rebellions were mere naughtiness: stealing his parents' whisky, sometimes crushing in one hand one of the worthless ornaments that invigilated his prison. It was the ordinariness of those day-to-day misdemeanours that struck me. This wasn't the break-out, the over-turning, the *gran rifiuto* that he had encouraged. It had nothing of the cultivated soul, who rises above constraints and laws and conventions only to endorse them from a point of unshriven transgression, who feels in his innermost self the pain of the cosmic order that he also betrays. The crazy thing was that I should have attributed such a stance to Bill, as he passed between the back door and the front door of his parents' house or sat enthroned in their garage inventing himself as a fiction in order not to live among facts.

I decided to put off my initiation into *Tristan*. I formed the habit of walking around the block to the bus-stop, avoiding Bill's house. But for all my rebellion against him, Bill was ever-present within me, urging me, guiding me, prising me loose from the world. I was still a character in one of his stories, con-fined by the inverted commas that he had planted around my life. I spent my afternoons in the German section of the public library, reading in translation the authors whom he had recom-mended, not daring to take the volumes home lest I should fall forever under their spell, but confining them to a corner of my dull existence. It was on a chill October afternoon, rooting through the shelves and thinking with self-dramatizing grief of Linda's kisses, that I came across Oswald Spengler's *Decline of the West*. Curious, I took down the first volume and opened it at random. Here was what I read:

One day the last portrait of Rembrandt and the last bar of Mozart will have ceased to be—though possibly a coloured canvas and a sheet of notes may remain—because the last eye and the last ear accessible to their message will have gone.

The words were simple, but they astonished me. I embraced the idea at once, as though it had always unconsciously been mine. The culture I had grasped from Bill and Dr. Jackson was destined to disappear, had already vanished except from those small private places, like Bill's drab living room, where its after-image lingered in eyes that had turned from the universal conflagration so as to shine into the dark. And as I leafed through those pages that purported to summarize the history of all civilizations, and to show the parallel destiny of each of them in decay and death, a kind of exhilarating grief arose within me. The book was addressed directly and personally to me, linking my emotions to the destiny of the world. I was caught up in a drama of untold proportions and, just as the worshipper leaps to discover God's personal interest in him; just as the psychoanalytic patient feels a renewed will to live on learning that his petty suffering conforms to some universal archetype; so did I become happy in my mournful emotions, knowing that it was not I, but culture itself, that was alive in them, and also dying there.

I borrowed the book, and read through the night. Seldom had I been gripped as I was gripped by that opening chapter, in which mathematics is thrown from its pedestal. Mathematics, the heart of my studies, the paradigm of certainty, the foundation of science, was promoted from science to culture, and then dashed to the floor. The "Faustian" mathematics of the West, set beside the "Magian" mathematics of Arabia and the "Apollonian" mathematics of Euclid, appeared neither more nor less valid than they. It ceased to be an objective science and became instead an expression of the Faustian spirit that lives and thrives in all the great creations of our culture, and whose death-pangs had been foretold in me. Spengler granted a vision above science, above fact, above theory and knowledge, a vision that made me privy to the meaning of the world. And the strange thing was that this final proof that Western culture must die, was all but dead already, attached me the more firmly to it, made me determined to store within myself the precious heritage, and take it with me to the grave. In those early morning hours of a damp October day in a suburban street in Surrey, I became a mystic, a prophet of doom, and a German.

Except for the squads of motorcycles that occasionally roared through our streets, the nights were silent. From time to time I would look up from my desk in the attic bedroom, and stare at the houses opposite, silhouetted against the yellow glare from the Croydon suburbs. In a week I was to take my Cambridge entrance exam. After that I would be gone from here—fleeing in the cold dawn light and leaving only a note for my parents. And a thousand crazy schemes rushed through my mind—I would live rough on London streets, work my passage on a cargo ship, join a bank like T.S. Eliot, or find some noble protector. And I would carry within me the secret knowledge that, wherever I was, I did not belong.

Immersed again in Spengler it was some time before I took note of the soft steady padding of footsteps in the street below. It was four in the morning, and the suburb slumbered in its blank repose. But someone patrolled beneath my window, someone anxious and sleepless and alone. It could not be Bill, since a screen of psychic electricity prevented him from straying more than a hundred yards from his house. Therefore it was Linda, penitent and full of yearning, escaped from her Oxford college to beg forgiveness. This idea grew so quickly and strongly that it was soon irresistible, and, not daring to disprove it by leaning from the window, I crept down the stairs, past the perfumed mausoleum where my parents slept, to the hallway, where the street-light cast a shadow against the frosted glass of the door.

It was the shadow of a man, tall, thin, and bald, who raised his hands above his head in a posture of defence. Lest he should knock and wake my parents, I quickly took my coat from the rack in the hallway and went into the street.

"We must begin from the assumption that all conceivable weapons have been used," Bill whispered. His lips trembled and his eyes stared wildly past me into the dark interior of our house. "You are therefore no longer capable of hurting me."

I walked quickly away from the house and he followed me.

"Don't think you can run away from me. I shall always be there. I made you, Michael Sillitoe, I won't let you forget it, I made you."

He was speaking more loudly, using words that were unutterable in a street like ours. I hurried on in anguish. A hundred yards from our house there stood an old transformer station, behind which a footpath between back gardens led to a piece of common ground. This ground contained no roads or lights or houses, only the debris of human reproduction: prams, fridges, and cycle frames among the thorns. If I could reach it I would be safe, and the tirade that was just beginning would spend itself unheard. But the narrow footpath permitted only a single file, and Bill, following close behind, was impatient to be heard.

"Whatever you know that's worth knowing, you know because of me. Don't deny it Michael Sillitoe. You're a shit, do you hear? A snivelling little bourgeois little suburban little shit, spick and span little normal little righteous little tit-fondling cunt-coveting shit, a prayerful, pastoral, piss-artistic, Pan-pessimistic prig of a shit..."

Whatever the value of culture, it is more or less useless in a crisis. Words said in jealous anger come from deeper down, are smeared with the rotting compost of our early years, and are vomited into the conversation as proof of our foul insides. I hated Bill, and also feared him. I mumbled at him to lower his voice, to wait till we could talk, to have some respect. But it only made things worse.

"Ho ho!" he roared. "I am to wash my mouth out, drink rose water and balsamic oils, smear orrery and potash on my crumbling teeth, have my tongue sent to the cleaners, book myself in for a larynx by-pass, maybe a heart and soul by-pass, so that Michael Sillitoe will not be ashamed in front of the neighbours!"

A dog barked nearby, and then another. The footpath was dark and my feet were splashing in unseen ruts and puddles. Bill reached out to take hold of my sleeve, but I snatched it away from him and hurried on. We reached the common, where the yellow glow of the suburban night shone on our faces, and I turned to him.

"You're to leave me alone, O.K.? I have my life to lead, see? I've got exams next week for God's sake!"

He laughed at this, and I wasn't surprised. Whatever excuse I made would merely trace a path away from him. He shook his head and chuckled mirthlessly.

"Michael, Michael," he said with mocking gentleness. He spread his arms to either side, and then let them flap against the long black overcoat he wore, as though to illustrate the futility of all embraces. I felt no pity for him: I was young, frightened, my life had not begun; all I wanted was out. Escape became the order of the day—escape not from Bill only, but from the place and the time that contained him.

"Listen Bill. I'm serious. Of course I'm grateful for everything. But I can't give you what you want. It's right off the agenda."

He stared at me and began to pant rhythmically.

"You don't know what I want. You don't care what I want. What do you think it's like, being me? Have you ever asked yourself? Ten years of darkness, and now the doors closing again. Just tell me her name, for Christ's sake!"

His face in the yellow half-light seemed eaten away, clinging in tatters to the skull, and the eyes were caverns of darkness. I tried to hide my disgust, and he started towards me, his chest heaving and sobbing, his hands tearing at my clothes. I struggled to free myself, but he held my arms in an iron grip and shook me, howling like a dog into my face. I took a quick decision.

"She's irrelevant," I said. "She's gone. Listen Bill. Just give me a week—it's all I ask. Then we can work things out."

He stopped howling and released my arms.

"Oh, of course we can work things out," he said. "And you'll come round just as you always did, and maybe—"

He broke off with a frightened stare.

"Where are we Michael? How did we come here? Oh God, I've got to get back!"

He was already running towards the footpath. I watched him but I did not follow. Then he stopped and turned, his mouth open, his hands flapping about his head.

"Michael! Michael! Help me!"

He sank to his knees in the mud, his upturned face gasping for air. Still I felt no pity for him, and although I was scandalized by my heartlessness, I made no move towards him. I was schooling myself to reject all responsibility for Bill. He was over and done with.

Bill was sobbing now, his face in his hands, the shining cap of his skull bobbing up and down like a ball in water. I went slowly over to him.

"Get up now Bill. You must go home."

He glanced up at me from eyes boiling with tears.

"Hard is the descent to God," he said. "But he's there, waiting. I'll reach him soon. I'll rescue him. Just trust me Michael."

He shook his head sadly, then rose to his feet. As I led the way down the footpath to our street, he followed meekly, head bowed and hands heavy at his sides. A few lights had come on in the windows. Someone pulled back the curtains in the house next to Bill's. I guided him by the elbow on to the gravel driveway. He turned back to me.

"And then, when the exams are over, you'll come round for *Tristan*? Maybe next Wednesday? It's a whist evening. They'll be out."

"Of course. Next Wednesday. I promise. And I'll do some homework first, so that you won't need to explain everything."

"Thank you Michael," he said, as he walked away.

But we never did listen to *Tristan*. For a week I shut Bill from my mind, applied myself to study, travelled to Cambridge, and returned, the exam over, with a simulacrum of resolve. I went round to Bill's on the Wednesday not to hear *Tristan* but to say goodbye. But he had got there first. The door was opened by his mother, a middle-aged lady in a stiff blue suit, with a thin stiff face like a nurse. She did not look at me directly, nor did she invite me in.

"I'm afraid Bill's not here," she said. "You must be Michael."

I agreed with that much at least.

"He's gone, you see."

Her voice was without expression, as though announcing the news on the radio.

"Where to?"

"Oh well, you see, he kept falling down. The doctor said he should see a specialist. So we took him to the hospital."

"Which hospital?"

"Saint Thingamejig's, I keep forgetting the name, over the other side of Croydon. But you see, they don't want visitors. Not yet."

She sounded relieved. Clearly the decision had been made to erase Bill from the family archive. I hesitated for a moment, searching for an appropriate remark.

"Well," I said. "If you talk to him, tell him I came round."

"Yes, I'll tell him that," she said, with a nod of the head, as though glad of the inspiration.

I walked back slowly to our house, with a strange hollow feeling, as though life had suddenly run out of me. That Friday the local paper carried the headline: "Mental patient falls from hospital roof." The description of the dead man left no doubt that it was Bill. My only thought as I read was to wonder how he could have climbed up there. Surely security was not so lax?

The letter of acceptance from Cambridge came four days later. During those days I had kept to my room, neither reading nor thinking nor feeling, like a creature waiting to be born. The news from Cambridge awoke me. I took my passport, savings book, some clothes, and a copy of Rilke's poems and left one morning before dawn. The note on the kitchen table promised a letter every month, but gave no explanation. For I had no explanation.

Nor do I remember much of those nine months of wandering. Some things, scenes, and faces, come back to me. And there was one serious affair—at least, I suppose it was serious, since it lasted several months—long enough for me to learn German from Ulrike, who was a student in Düsseldorf, and who fed me and housed me in that dreary town until I left without a goodbye in the middle of her exams. I did not mean to be heartless; I did not mean to be anything—meaning and being were both on hold, as I drifted in a kind of sealed vacuum through foreign parts and strange attachments. I earned money here and there—muck-spreading on an industrialised farm near Hanover, dishwashing in a restaurant in Kessel, playing twelve-bar blues in a Düsseldorf Biergarten—which is how I met Ulrike. And I sent a postcard home each month, with a somnambulistic greeting. But inside me was a uniform blankness—a vast flat desert, beneath the surface of which strange things were constantly shifting and adjusting. Fear, horror, grief and guilt had all sped away in the relentless glare of nothingness. And when I read in Heidegger that *das Nichts nichtet*—that Nothing noths—I knew exactly what he meant, and cherished the thought as my own.

For I was still reading, immersing myself in the past—not the past of England, but the past of Germany, whose ghosts had been walled in behind towers and tenements, whose pavements cringed beneath my feet with their buried secrets, whose people sped into the future with empty faces, like blank sheets of paper in the wind. Ulrike had been baptised Magdalena but had renamed herself after the terrorist Ulrike Meinhof. She believed that Germany would rise again only when the ruling class had been decimated, in acts of exemplary violence. To me it didn't seem much of an improvement on the Nazi view. But I observed her from behind a screen. I was never close to her, not even in bed, and curiosity played only a small part in our relations. Ulrike wanted it that way. She had a business-like approach to things, and would calculate the number of murders needed to destroy the bourgeoisie with the same bureaucratic pedantry that she applied to writing an essay on social statistics or exploring scientific sex in accordance with the newly published manual of Dr. Comfort. She accepted me as a factor in her calculations, was pleased that I had no feelings, and allowed me to drift beside her, just out of reach.

Not that I was always with her. On the contrary, I wandered for weeks at a time, taking my books and a sleeping-bag, hitching lifts, living rough, eating rye bread and sausage in the streets of ugly towns whose names I never learned, watching the life which is no life of a nation that has lost its memory, and been forbidden to mourn. I read the German classics, explored museums and cathedrals, studied Burckhardt and Ranke, and conjured corny pictures of the vanished Germany with which to compare the present void. I became something of an alienation expert, moving from place to place in search of nowhere, mingling with the crowds as they played moronic games in stadiums, and sitting among whey-faced youths as they pumped their veins with heroin in the public parks. Time stood still for me—whole days would pass in which I thought nothing, observed nothing, felt nothing save the blistering rays of Nothing in my soul.

Only one part of me seemed to grow during those vacant months, and that was my love of music. The Düsseldorf Marxists were disco-fans, and Ulrike was no exception. Disco formed the background to everything she did, and her bedroom was plastered with pictures of her favourite lesbian trio: the Bo-Bo Girls, whose costume was black leather, bare nipples, dark glasses and Kalashnikovs. Had Ulrike fulfilled her greatest ambition and gunned down a judge in front of his family, it would have been with a Walkman on her ears and the Bo-Bo Girls singing their hit number, *"Ich hasse dich."* Everywhere in Germany I heard the jug-a-jug rhythm and tuneless monody of disco, and this reinforced the sense of my apartness—as though I had been elected to remember the musical tradition that these barbarians refused to inherit. The judgement was snobbish and unfair: but how was I to know that I was not the distinguished exception I took myself to be, but merely one among millions, most of them German, who heard with impotent outrage this all-pervasive antidote to music and grieved in their hearts that the greatest achievement of their civilisation was soon to be lost?

Ulrike lived in a block of flats, two miles from the centre, next to a Technische Hochschule. The school had a Bechstein grand, standing in a wide-windowed hall full of dust and chalk and the group smell of children. The old janitor—a mild man with twinkling blue eyes and a grey moustache, who had doubtless been a loyal Nazi when loyal Nazis were required— allowed me to play the piano after hours. There was a cupboard containing sheet music, and when I was not sleep-walking through the ruined landscape of Germany, I was fixed to this spot. Beyond the tall wide windows everything was blank and incomprehensible. Here, in this place that was visited outside school hours only by me and by God, I re-discovered the inner life. I came to know the sonata repertoire. I played through two-hand reductions of the Beethoven symphonies, and vocal scores of the Mozart operas. I rediscovered Bach, and felt what must have been my only spasm of real emotion during those months of nothingness.

One evening, fighting my way through the first E-flat minor fugue, there arose within me the image of Dr. Jackson in his scuffed old tweeds as he leaned across me at the keyboard. He had showed me how that innocent theme works its way through inversions and elaborations to its final statement in double time, becoming defiant and dignified without losing its childlike simplicity and ineffable sadness. For him it was the musical image of honesty, which is why he called it Cordelia, and there was a kind of confession in his voice when he said this. I imagined a forlorn and adolescent love, to the memory of which he had consecrated his celibate existence. And recalling Dr. Jackson in that empty hall in Düsseldorf, as the summer storm-clouds gathered outside, and a thin shaft of sunlight brushed my fingers on the keyboard, I dissolved in tears. For a whole hour I wept, not knowing for whom or why. And the strange thing is that, while I thought of Dr. Jackson, of Linda, of the Church at Etticombe, even of my parents and their dormant being, I did not think of Bill. Not once during my months in Germany. Not thinking about Bill was an unconscious policy, my body's way of getting through.

And the policy lasted through my first year at Cambridge, a year spent sleep-walking between lecture-rooms and libraries. I had been admitted to read natural sciences, specialising in biochemistry. But I changed at once to English, less for the subject's sake than for the ease with which I could ignore it. Indifferent to politics, I joined no debating society, no discussion group, no political movement. Without talent for the theatre, and with only an amateur competence at the piano, I kept my culture to myself, hiding from my contemporaries the inner thoughts that secretly distanced me from them. For more than a year I strove to be as like my college neighbours as I could, imitating by turns their Rod Stewart haircuts, their Bob Dylan posters, their desks piled with fanzines, their Rasta dialogue. I learned bass guitar, and even joined an amateur pop group, playing sequences that kicked their way into my soul like gangs of hooligans, but whose stupidity I would have denied if need be under torture.

Real music was my guilty secret. I would listen to it alone in the middle of the day, after my neighbours had left for their lectures, when a kind of sultry domesticity reigned on our staircase, and the drab girlfriends of the night before rose one by one from their sheets to pad around the bathroom.

I hid my culture even from my supervisor—a dreary Marxist called Hargreaves, who lived in the Eastern suburbs among nappies and toys and back issues of the *New Left Review*, and who associated English literature, English history, English art and music, and the very idea of England, with the class oppression symbolized by Cambridge. It was thanks to Dr. Hargreaves that I ended my first year with a dissertation of consummate fatuousness on the Liverpool Poets, having written essays on Barthes, Saussure, and Kristeva, meticulously reproducing the Parisian gobbledygook prescribed for the course in "literary theory," and adding faint sarcastic asides about the poverty of English literature and the madness of Dr. Leavis. All this I did in a state of denial. For there, right in the centre of my psyche, was the place where Bill sat wrapped in grief, waiting like some Homeric ghost for the blood that would once again bring life and love and understanding.

Then one day, on a dank November afternoon in my second year, after I had changed my course of study yet again, I came across an article in the *Allgemeine Musikalischer Zeitung* of 1928, on Spengler and Schoenberg. I sat in a cubicle, high up in the University Library tower. The window overlooked the Backs, and the afternoon mist was rising from the river Cam, veiling the colleges, and curling around the finials on the roof of King's College chapel—that majestic structure which had sailed proudly from the age of faith, to run aground in a place of treachery. The scene had a peculiar Cambridge melancholy—the melancholy of celibate dreams and stone-built isolation, of collegiate solitude and the chill damp air of the fens. And it blended in my thoughts with the text that lay open before me.

Written in a formal, stilted German, the article angrily repudiated the twelve-tone system, as the triumph of "civilisation" over "culture." This regimented, mathematical, law-governed, and unfeeling system, the author wrote, was the enemy of natural music—the music that arises spontaneously in the culture of a people, and which expresses their will to live, to propagate, to claim the world as their own. And the author referred approvingly to Spengler, whose thesis that civilisation begins when culture dies, seemed to contain a warning addressed to the entire German nation. Nor did he neglect Schoenberg's Jewishness, and the "Magian" spirit that expressed itself through this alien music. The Faustian soul of Western man, the author wrote, soars free and with infinite aspiration in the *endlose Melodie* of Wagner, but is enslaved and humiliated by serialism, which, with Talmudic finickiness, binds the soul of music in its chains. The doom-laden thoughts seemed to rise from the page, to mingle with the Cambridge mist, and to pour their poison over the world beyond the window. And suddenly I recalled that damp October morning back home when, my head full of this same intoxicating nonsense, wanting the disaster cherished by Spengler to be my disaster too, I had heard the unceasing footsteps in the street below. And I remembered that it was not Spengler or Eliot or any of my cultural heroes who had made me conscious of the twilight, but Bill, whose belief in the end was also an inward determination to resist it; and I discovered that I had loved and admired him right up to that moment when I opened the door to find him strung like a puppet from the dawn sky.

I was overcome by remorse. Had it not been for my coldness of heart, Bill would have been alive and on the road to recovery, perhaps visiting me in Cambridge and taking pleasure in my studies. It was Bill who had deflected me from science, who had offered culture as my icon, who had shown me that our world can be known and understood through music. It was to Bill that I owed my decision first to read English, and then to change after a year to music, maybe one day to pursue an academic career. And it was Bill's obscure remark about Mahler that had awoken me to the life of the mind.

I remembered Bill's head, his fragile cranium and taut translucent skin, the long prehensile fingers moving above it as though exploring a halo of pain, and I was astonished to think that I could have been frightened of him, that I could have responded to him with something other than admiring and pitying affection. And yes, it is possible to admire what you also pity: Nietzsche was wrong about this, as he was wrong about everything, as wrong and corrupting as Spengler.

I left my books in the library and walked with a strange new wakefulness towards my college digs on Jesus Green. I packed up my books and clothes, and telephoned home. I was leaving Cambridge, I said. Probably I would work in London; maybe go for a job in publishing. My parents, who understood this decision no more than they understood all the other events and non-events that had destroyed their timid hopes for me, nevertheless listened with meek surrender, and agreed to fetch me in the car. Conversation had long since died between us, and the silent journey around London was filled with my mourning for Bill. Only one thing could help me, which was to make contact with him somehow, to fight for him, to see him rise again within me, offering his forgiveness.

My bedroom at home sickened me. The school clothes in the wardrobe were somehow shamefaced, as though I had caught them in the act of being just the same, going over and over in privacy and darkness the rituals that I had chosen not to remember. The stale odour of guilt still clung to them, and I shut the door on them as though concealing a crime. I moped for a day or so, reading nothing, occasionally walking past Bill's house, where china dogs stood in their old position in the window, framed by the same mustard-coloured curtains of a vaguely abstract design. Then I came across an advertisement in our local paper from a rehabilitation centre for the mentally ill, asking for volunteers. I arranged an interview and arrived at the Victorian red-brick building in Croydon in a serious mood, eager to do for a stranger what I had refused to do for Bill.

I was shown into a large bright office which, but for its size, resembled the rooms of my Cambridge neighbours. A large poster of the Beach Boys had been stuck with blue tacks to the wall above a long modern desk piled high with football magazines. A low coffee table stood in the middle of the room, bearing a squash racket, a can of Newcastle Brown, and a copy of a body-building magazine. A metal filing cabinet stood against one wall, its side covered with stickers from the Socialist Workers' Party, and its drawers lying open and empty. The large sash window gave on to a pleasant street of Victorian houses, with white stucco facades and pollarded lime trees. There was a faint smell of stale cigarette smoke—so faint, however, as to suggest a previous occupant, who had moved on from this place, as everyone did in time. Furniture, equipment, decoration, even smell seemed provisional, temporary, without the burdens of ownership or purpose. I stood alone in the room, and the light seemed to expand around me. The crazy impression arose that this was my home, that I belonged here, that this would be the centre of my existence. I pictured myself coming each day into that light-filled centre, from which my good works would radiate outwards over a grateful world. I belonged here, where none had belonged.

A young man entered and greeted me with a short self-confident "Hi!" He was stocky, shabbily dressed in jeans and dun-coloured cardigan, with unkempt red hair and a faint sprinkling of beard. His pouchy blue eyes fixed me for a moment, and then wandered towards the desk. A row of silver earrings in his left ear caught the light from the window, and twinkled above the punctured skin, which was white, lifeless, and cheesy.

"So you want to help us," he said. "That's good. Do you realize what you're taking on?"

I began to reassure him, but he interrupted me.

"I mean, do you realize what a state we're in? It's just incredible. The country is falling apart. Rampant capitalism. Greed. Profiteering. Wherever you look, just self, self, self. What do you make of it?"

"Well, I suppose I..."

"The incredible thing is, nobody cares. Just a few of us, working at the bottom of the pile, trying to pick up the pieces. But only a temporary measure. It's like putting plaster on a flesh-wound, when the insides have been shot to bits. What this country needs is a—fuck, someone's been at my papers."

He was sifting through the pile of football mags, extracting letters, scraps of paper, and what seemed like closely typed minutes of a meeting. After a moment's agitation, he settled down again to his theme, standing at the desk with his back to me, and turning every now and then with a rapid and unfriendly glance.

"We need volunteers. Oh yes, we need volunteers. But not the do-gooders, the charity-mongers, the beautiful souls who prop up the system so that suffering goes on. That's the trouble with this country. Charity. Good causes. Lady Bountiful. Royal visitors, picking their dainty way through shattered lives. And the politicians, telling us we should get off our butts, take responsibility for our lives, play up and play the game. Do you know something?"

He turned towards me with a venomous look, and I tried to appear seriously fascinated by his diagnosis of our social ills.

"The really sick people in this country are up there on top, shouting for nuclear bombs, armies, police-forces, punishments, perks for their friends, while pissing on the poor sods who have to carry the can. And when people decide they can't take any more of it, and try to live a half-way decent life, they are diagnosed as schizophrenics and locked away—or else handed over to us, for rehabilitation. 'Rehabilitation'—I ask you! Teaching the buggers to keep their heads down, putting them out of our misery! It's positively obscene. I'll tell you some-thing'—and he shot another angry look in my direction—'it's not our clients who need to be fitted into this society; it's society that needs to be fitted round our clients. They're the ones who have paid the price, the heroes, the martyrs. Are you queer?"

"Well, I—not really."

"Pity. What our clients need is self-confidence. They think there must be something wrong with them, because they have the feeling they're wading knee-deep in shit. But they *are* wading knee-deep in shit, and we should tell them so. What's your name anyway?"

"Michael Sillitoe."

"Look, Michael, you're not the right person for this job, you realize that? You're too young. You have been going up the ladder, rung by rung. When did you freak out?"

"I don't think I ever *did* freak out."

"There you are. You can't hope to empathize with our clients when you are totally cut off from their experience. I've always said this to the Council. But they go on sending the wrong recruits. What the hell do they think they're playing at? And they call themselves socialists."

He threw the paper back on to the coffee table and looked at me more mildly.

"No offence. But we should be clear where we stand. Sit down for a moment, if you like."

He gestured to a shabby armchair with bentwood arms and a brown flock cover, pitted with cigarette-burns. I hesitated and then decided to sit, if only to show my cool.

"I'm Jerry," he said, and remained standing before me, looking down on me with a sudden curiosity, as though recognising a long-lost friend. "I have probably been in this job longer than is good for me. When did you say you freaked?"

"I didn't."

He laughed abruptly, and his pudgy face crumpled, as though pressed to a window.

"Of course you did. It's written all over you. People don't come here to *offer* help. They come to receive it. They want to spend time with the really ruined, the really broken and buggered and beaten down, so as to convince themselves they're coping. Do you think you're coping?"

"Not very well," I admitted.

"No. It's not surprising. You remind me of someone actually. He used to come here five years ago, when I was new to the job. He had been sacked from a solicitors' office, described himself as a writer, spent whole days in the centre here, creeping about in a broken kind of way, conducting imaginary symphonies, humming to himself, and once in a while shouting 'Beethoven' at the top of his voice. Cambridge graduate. Pretended he had come to help. Would give long speeches, addressed to no one in particular, about the ruin of modern culture, and how we could all live again thanks to Beethoven. When I told him I prefer disco he said 'what else do you expect from a schizophrenic?' The culture illusion, I call it. Loads of people suffer from it. And they imagine they come here to help us!

"Yeah man," he went on. "There's no special distinction in being fucked up. The only difference is between those who admit it and those who don't."

He leered at me from his puffy eyes and gave a complicitous nod. I searched for words, but none would come. The armoury of culture proved as useless to me as it had been to Bill. Those antiquated words and old allusions stayed fixed to the wall of my mind like rusty weapons, trophies from some small-scale private triumph that would be laughable in a modern battle. Ulrike had a way of closing the trigger on an imaginary submachine gun whenever I tried to put my case. "*Waffnen, nicht Worte*," she would say: weapons, not words, as though words were a thing of the past for her, like marriage, string quartets, and religion.

I noticed a little wooden Snoopy doll half hidden by the beer can on the table. It had a cheeky satirical expression, as though designed to reduce all encounters in this room to the level of farce. I reached out to pick it up and began to play with it in my hand. A grey light descended on the ugly furniture, a light of mourning. Everything in the room seemed discarded. It was a place at the end of life; like a transit camp where prisoners die among junk, cut off from all that they need and love. As I played with the little doll, I seemed to hear Bill's voice again, his urgent imperatives, and behind them the barely hidden need for my acceptance. I imagined him fighting for his hard-won right to exist in this very room, with this very person, and everything sinking away inside, as it had sunk away in the face of my rejection.

"You see, I knew that man," I said. "And yes, he is dead. Maybe you should feel a little guilty."

I got up and faced him, passing the little doll from hand to hand, and debating whether I should throw it. He turned to the desk.

"Guilty!" he said, with a laugh.

He reached for the telephone and pressed a button on the

keypad.

"Jim?" he said. "Difficult client here. Might need your help. Thanks."

He replaced the receiver and came slowly towards me.

"One thing you learn in this job, Michael, is not to feel guilt. People come to us with guilt. It oozes from every pore. I mean, just look at you! We offer help, see. And that means staying out of the guilt game."

The door opened, and two burly men in overalls entered. Jerry calmly moved aside, picked up the beer can and drank from it. One of the men pinned my arms to my side while the other prized my fingers free from the Snoopy doll, as though taking a toy from a child.

"I should think," Jerry continued, wiping his mouth, "that you'll be sitting on the pavement somewhere in a couple of minutes time in a real orgy of guilt. I expect you'll be crying your eyes out over that freak we tried to help. And you'll know that it's not our fault at all, but yours. Because that's the long and short of it. Whenever there's a question of guilt, the guilt is yours. Bah!"

He tossed the can into a corner of the room and walked out. I followed him, lifted off my feet and carried like a sack of unwanted goods into the street. And yes, Jerry was right. I did sit on the pavement for a while. And I did weep a little, not for Bill only, but for all the hopes and dreams that he had awoken in me, and which had followed him into the grave. And as I sat there, leaning against a low brick wall, a queasy feeling came over me. I felt the annihilating flow of time, and the steady erasure of the past. Bill's love for me was past, and therefore unreal, even impossible. It was a Now that had flickered and gone out. He sat enthroned in a fictional garage, not an actual garage but a sedan chair of possibilities, which had crumbled to nothing as the world moved on. The mystery of time and the mystery of Bill were one: and he was gone as time had gone and England had gone. There was nothing left of him save footfalls echoing in the memory, down the passage that we did not take.

Two days later I called on Bill's parents. It was strange to be standing once again beneath that familiar street-lamp, to be lifting the latch on the wrought-iron gate, to be walking on the crazy-paving between neatly tonsured lawns, to be ringing the bell, hearing its two saccharine chimes, and peering at the blown-glass panel in the door, in which the vague shadows of human movement swam like half glimpsed fish. I had decided to confront them, to explain what I had lost in losing Bill, to force them somehow to make amends, by making amends myself. I imagined a trunk of manuscripts. I could be Bill's editor, rescuing him from the sea of forgetting and polishing his corpse by the shore. And in entertaining these plans I felt a surge of distaste for Bill's parents, so that, as the shadow of a man troubled the glass in front of me, I directed towards it all the anger that I should have directed at myself. I imagined Bill's father as he opened the door, the complacent blankness of his face giving way to fear, then grief and finally remorse on seeing me. A hand turned the latch, and through the gap between door and jamb came the faint white sound of modern jazz.

"You've been a long time getting in touch," said Bill, "assuming it's really you."

He was dressed in a dark suit, with the tie loose about his neck. A trim moustache softened the lines of his mouth, and lank hairs were smoothed over his yellowish cranium. He stared for a moment at my astonished face and then quickly looked away.

"But I thought..."

"Come in, have a chat."

Bill stepped back and made a sweeping gesture with his left arm, of a kind that I had never seen in him before. He no longer stooped, and his thin face had an almost babyish shine to it, as though he had been rubbing it with cream. I followed Bill to the living room, where he promptly crossed to the record player and lifted the needle from the disk.

"Always calms me down," he said, then added without looking up, "though I don't suppose it has the same effect on you."

"Bill..."

"Just a minute."

He retreated into the kitchen, where he passed a moment of silence before returning. His breath, as he neared me, smelt of whisky.

"So, Michael," he said slowly, "how's Cambridge?"

Outside there was a squeal of brakes. Bill started and an anxious expression crossed his face. For a moment I glimpsed, behind the moustache, the frail, suffering creature I had known. And then he resumed his sarcastic smile and went to the window.

"Bill, I... I thought you were dead."

"I'm not so easily disposed of."

"They told me they had taken you to the hospital, and then I read that a patient had fallen from the roof of St Margaret's. I was certain it was you..."

"St Margaret's? You mean the loony bin? For heaven's sake! OK, that's where I should have been. But all I had was an ear infection. And you see, I survived."

He stood in the window, and began to whistle beneath his breath what sounded like a long saxophone solo. I had sat down by now, trying to take in what had happened. It was as though my mistake had killed off the old Bill and brought into being a newer model, more fitted to suburban life, and more proof against disaster. I asked what he was doing. Speaking in a matter of fact tone and not looking in my direction, he described his work as a conveyancing clerk. The office where he spent his days was in the church close, next to Dr Jackson's cottage. Sometimes he saw Dr. Jackson; in fact they had become friends, and would drink a pint together after office hours each Friday.

"Of course," Bill said, "his Anglican prissiness gets on my nerves, as do Elgar, VW, blue remembered hills, et cetera." He gave a snort, and turned in my direction. "But he helped me, Michael, just as you did. When you disappeared like that, not saying to anyone how to find you, and yet still connected to me by plans and promises and a thread of what you could almost call passion, if that wasn't too antique a word, I had to face an existential question. Do I carry on with this pretence called culture, even though there is no one now to poison with it? Or do I return to an abnormal life? You see the problem."

Suddenly he stood to attention and let out a gust of laughter. It lasted too long to be an expression of amusement and indeed had something contrived and theatrical about it. He stared from his hooded eyes, not at me, but at some object clinging to the wall behind me.

"You didn't poison me, Bill. You gave me a life."

I told him how I had been changed by his instruction, abandoning science to study first English and then music, all the while living from the idea of culture that he had first planted in my thoughts. He looked at me with appalled disgust, and then, for the first time, made one of his old familiar gestures, raising his hands to his ears and beating off the imaginary birds that had begun to assemble there.

"Look," he said at last. "That's not a life you're describing. It's a sickness. When I suffered from it, I couldn't move from this place, not further than the end of the road. Now I can get to the office and back. I talk to my parents. I earn money. I have friends—maybe. And when the telly is on I sit and watch it, just like everybody else. Anyway, why did you come here if you thought I was dead?"

I had no answer to his question, save to look mournfully at the carpet. Bill really was dead: I had made no mistake. But his cause too had died with him. I rose to go, and he did not detain me. As I shut the front gate I looked briefly back at the window. Bill was clutching his hands in front of him, facing the street with a look of unspeakable anguish. And then he saw me and laughed.

Author photo by Pete Helme

ABOUT THE AUTHOR

ROGER SCRUTON is a freelance writer and philosopher, who rescued himself from the academy twenty years ago. He currently lives in rural Wiltshire, England. He has held posts in the American Enterprise Institute, and in the Ethics and Public Policy Center. He is married with two children. He is the author of 40 books, including five works of fiction, and composed two operas. He is widely known on both sides of the Atlantic as a public intellectual with a broadly conservative vision. His acclaimed novel about communist Czechoslovakia, *Notes from Underground*, was published by Beaufort Books in 2014.